Futures

A collection

By

Mark Bilsborough

Walks *Through* Walls

Click originally appeared in **Cover of Darkness** (Jan 12)
Spirit originally appeared in **Nebula Rift** (Mar 13)
For Hannah originally appeared in **Phantaxis** (Aug 17)
Immersion originally appeared in **Strange Fictions** (Jan 18)
Twins originally appeared in **K-Zine** (Sep 18)
Sideways originally appeared in **Storyteller** (May 17)
Hunter originally appeared in **Ray Gun Revival** (Mar 12)
Certainty originally appeared in **Perihelion SF** (Mar 14)
Valentine's Dilemma originally appeared in **On the Premises** (Apr 17)

First published in the UK by **Walks *Through* Walls** 2020

ISBN: 978-1-8381529-6-3

Contents

Foreword

Futures is a collection of near-future science fiction stories, most of them originally published in a variety of magazines and online publications. They're what-ifs rather than predictions – I don't even know what I'm going to have for lunch today yet – but because they're *near* future, I'm making a few pretty shrewd guesses.

Take the world of *Valentine's Dilemma* and its sister story *The Beggar and the Golden Dome,* for instance, where global warming has made the land all but uninhabitable, and cities survive under protective dome while methane storms ravage the planet. Then there's love in the age of AI in *For Hannah,* where digital perfection competes with reality.

There's first contact in *Certainty,* refining our sense of identity in the light of our growing knowledge. Or a different kind of first contact in *Spirit,* which is a fishy take on alien abduction.

There's plenty of dystopia here too. *Mad Panic, Flying Paper and Philosopher Cats* is a sanguine take on the end of the world. More ambivalently, *Immersion* poses some difficult questions about our likely future use of virtual reality and *Twins* is framed by our capacity to blow things up.

Hunter takes us deeper into space and deeper into the future, but ironically it's probably the most 50s throwback in the collection, with the hero solving crimes the old fashioned way. *Click,* on the other hand, is a fast-paced VR action adventure, firmly rooted in the future.

The last two stories take us to the edge of the solar system and back. In *The Travelling Shakespeare Company*, members of a far flung mining colony orbiting Pluto gets more Shakespearian drama than they were anticipating take us And we round off with the poignant and ultimately optimistic *For Love.* set in the isolation of a deep space mission.

There isn't a consistent universe for these stories, but there are some common themes. Virtual reality is going to massively impact on our lives in years to come, as is AI. And at some point, we're going to have adjustment problems. Climate change impacts some of these stories and if anything I've probably downplayed its impact. And we still live with the threat of nuclear-powered destruction. Just because it hasn't happened, it doesn't mean the bombs aren't still out there.

The thread that binds them all is optimism. Life will be different. It'll be strange. We'll have to change, and that's going to be uncomfortable sometimes, but even at the end of the world the sun comes up in the morning, just like it always did. And we have a fighting chance of still being there to watch it.

Mark Bilsborough
Oct 2020

Valentine's Dilemma

Rena looked out over the devastation. Below her, East London's streets burned again, a pungent mix of fire and decay, threatening to overwhelm the dome's sensitive recycling systems.

Back in the old days she'd have put this down to plain and simple racial tension. She'd only just started her semi-regular visits to the area when the riots reached their heights, when whole rows of properties were firebombed. But that was a long time ago, before the weather got so bad that people had to start hiding underneath vast protective bubbles, safely watching in stunned amazement as the storms outside got ever more apocalyptic.

No, not race riots. This wasn't as focused as that, more an animal expression of frustration rather than fighting for a cause. The militia station had been the key target, which was just plain stupid. The response had been predictable: swift and brutal. The remaining rioters had then spent their time picking off easier targets—mainly each other.

Her companion turned to her. "This must be what the end of the world looks like."

Rena's crimson overalls were getting soot-blackened. She looked over at Valentine's still immaculate powder blue tunic and wondered how he did it. "That's a curious sentiment coming from you, Valentine. I thought you diagnostics took a slightly more measured view of events. I can fairly confidently say the end of the world is not yet nigh. Just a bit closer than yesterday."

They were standing on the roof of a tall building overlooking what used to be the East London Mosque, now the nerve centre of the dome's local government and militia. The rioters had attempted to overwhelm the building's force shield with a sustained beam attack, probably using weapons they'd put together on their kitchen tables. She could see some of them next to a scattering of blackened corpses. A couple of medium sized craters suggested someone had found something a lot more powerful to throw at the building, but the shield had held. That was predictable. Valentine was a diagnostic analyst. His job was to work out why the riot had happened. Rena's job, though, was to work out what might happen next.

Rena shivered. "Can we get back now?"

"With pleasure."

Rena and Valentine went straight to the coffee bar in the basement. Valentine winced as he took his first sip. "Don't know why I still drink this stuff. Never been the same since they started growing it in a cavern under Kew Gardens."

Rena looked at him closely. He was more nervous than usual, clearly dying to tell her something. "Something on your mind?"

Valentine shuffled in his seat and pulled at his ear. Rena had worked with him long enough to know that meant trouble. He took another sip. "Um, nothing. Probably. Look—you doing anything tonight?"

"You asking me out?"

Valentine gave a look which suggested the thought had never occurred to him. "Don't take this the wrong way, but no. I just want to take you to meet some people. A few things have happened that I need to get straight in my head."

"And I can help?"

"Let's just say I've learned to trust your judgment."

Rena was intrigued. Valentine dropped by her desk at seven o'clock and guided her out of the building. Twenty minutes later they were in a dingy Victorian bar near London Bridge. They were very close to the outer perimeter of the Westminster Dome and she found the distorting effect of the bubble at such close quarters unsettling.

Two men watched them from the other side of the bar, trying to look inconspicuous but failing badly. "Your friends don't seem very sure of us, Valentine."

"It's not me they're not sure about." Valentine strode off, returning a couple of minutes later and gesturing that they should move to a side room. The two people they'd seen at the bar were already there, together with a scruffily dressed woman with bright red hair.

"You sure about this, Valentine? We don't want any trouble," the shorter of the two men said. He was thickset, unhealthy looking.

"I'm vouching for her, aren't I? Rena, this is Evans." He pointed to the man who had spoken. "And this is Price."

They sat down. The woman spoke first. Rena noted no one had introduced her. "You're with Valentine? Didn't figure someone like you'd be his type. Too soft."

Rena's eyes narrowed.

"Well actually I'm an…"

"…old friend from college who used to get me to do outrageous things," Valentine interrupted "Still does."

Clearly they were undercover. Rena looked at the woman with growing curiosity. Something about her looked very familiar.

Despite her initial directness, the women orchestrated the conversation along slow, casual lines until, clearly having come to a decision, she leaned forward and abruptly changed the subject. "Tomorrow night, pub we were in last week, same time."

She pushed back on her chair, stood up and left. Evans and Price looked at each other, shrugged and followed, leaving Rena and Valentine alone.

"Valentine, was that who I think it was?"

He nodded. "Keris Edge. Thinks she can disguise herself with all that hair but she only has to open her mouth and she gives herself away."

"The urban terrorist Keris Edge?"

"The very same."

Rena sipped her beer quietly, taking it all in. "Then you're an urban terrorist too?"

"Do I look like an urban terrorist to you?"

"How would I know? Evans and Price looked like accountants. Talk."

And he did, in a roundabout way. But first they took a stroll along the South Bank, the Northern side of the Thames opposite them glowing gently with its subdued evening lighting. The air was, as always, calm and still and the ambient evening-controlled temperature ensured the embankment walkway was full. The crowd meant that the audio surveillance hookups would have difficulty making out what they were saying. Nevertheless, they kept their voices down.

"I came across her at a dinner party a couple of months ago. I recognized her straight away. She really does believe what she says, you know. That we're all going straight to hell."

"Lots of people believe that, Valentine. But most of them don't circulate a seditious underground newspaper."

He nodded. "But where she differs from all those people rioting in East London today is that she actually thinks our destiny is still in our hands. That we can do something about it."

"You've read it?"

"If you want to understand what's going on you have to ask questions and read some things the authorities might not like people looking at. Doesn't mean I have to agree with what's written."

"But you do, though, don't you?"

He nodded. "Some of it, yes. The bits about how we're all got our heads in the sand, pretending it's all business as usual."

"We prevail. We always do."

At that point they were passing the Tate Modern, brightly lit and very much open.

"It's easy to think that if you live and work in the Westminster Dome. Apart from the sky this place has hardly changed in decades. We're still got bars, restaurants, parks, museums and theatres. We can still go for a stroll at night and we can catch fish in the Thames. We're insulated from the nasty stuff outside."

Rena recalled that you never used to be able to catch fish in the Thames, back when it was a proper river flowing in from the outside. This walk always disturbed her, passing the site of Shakespeare's replica Globe Theatre before heading on to the Royal Festival Hall and the Ferris wheel outside the magnificent granite City Hall complex. The timeless permanence of this walkway contrasted sharply with her knowledge of the world outside. And the bomb crater across the river where Portcullis House used to be always brought her back to reality.

"But Keris doesn't think like that," he went on. "She's got a much clearer perspective. She grew up in the Central Manchester Dome. Was there right up until it collapsed."

"So, excellent source material for a diagnostic analyst like you."

"Exactly. I can learn more in one conversation with Keris than I can do in weeks talking to half dead rioters in East London."

"You've slept with her, haven't you?"

"Not the point."

"But it explains why she wasn't too keen to make friends with me back there."

"Don't get paranoid or take it personally. I should have realized she'd be spooked by anyone she hadn't personally vetted."

"How did she get here? I thought we'd completely cut Manchester off before the end."

No one quite knew what had happened in the Central Manchester Dome, only that it wasn't very pleasant. Rena realized Valentine would have been so intrigued by the prospect of talking to a survivor of that disaster that he would have completely disregarded the thought that there might be consequences of hanging out with a known and very wanted criminal.

"She survived in a sealed bomb shelter under militia HQ just before the final firestorm. She'd been one of the first to be arrested when the rioting started—any later and they'd just have shot her—and she was locked up in a holding cell in the basement when they sealed the floor."

"Rioting?"

"Claims she tried to stop it. Actually I believe her. After the smoke cleared and the rescue teams arrived from the neighbouring domes she was brought down here for questioning. They let her go when it became clear she wasn't really any part of what was going on."

"So what did happen?"

"Official report says a spontaneous dome breach let in a firestorm. But my best guess is a bomb. A big one. The dome ruptured in three places around the western edge and Keris' theory is that someone deliberately tried to tear the thing down. But before that all sorts of unpleasant stuff happened.

"Keris told me things had started to break down badly, coming to the end of their natural life. We hadn't got as far as we have now with hydroponics and underground farming when we put that dome together and Keris says the food began to run out. Then the temperature regulators started to fail. Keris told me the air got pretty stale by the end."

"So, classic end of the world riot."

"Something like that. Which is why I got so spooked in East London."

"And why you should know that we've got a long way to go yet. We've still got food, the air's still fresh and clean and providing you don't go around attacking militia stations life can be pretty good."

"Yes but it's not, is it? Ever so gradually, we're contracting in on ourselves. Fifty years ago there used to be sixty million people in this country, all arguing about whether global warming was real and driving their huge carbon-powered cars. Now there are fewer than a million, all penned into these perspex prisons. Thanks to the war we have a police state telling us what to think and what to do. Our work is assigned to us, our food is provided for us and our opinions are completely disregarded. You're the predictive analyst. You tell me which way things are going."

Rena shivered. "You know we need some discipline at the moment. Things were falling apart."

"Well self-interest was certainly destroying the planet. Trouble is, I'm not sure whether it was the self-interest of people trying to put petrol in their tanks or of politicians trying to justify their fancy positions."

They reached Westminster Bridge. On the other side of the river they could see the new Parliament building, more or less a replica of the one which was destroyed during the war, but with added gun turrets and an impenetrable security fence. Parliament only met twice a year these days, once for the King to open it and once for the MPs to sign everything off. Not that there was any real pretence at democracy any more. But still the building was majestic, a reminder that what was destroyed could be rebuilt, bigger and shinier than before. She was in no mood for Valentine's cynicism.

"Why did you bring me along tonight?"

They were halfway across the bridge before he answered. "Because I'm not quite as sure of things as you might think. I see bad things happening all around us and I dig down into the causes of those tragedies. And it's not hard to find them. A diagnostic analyst is basically a historian so I've seen this sort of thing many times before. It was easy for the authorities to justify this sort of suppression immediately after the war, but that doesn't make it right."

Rena was about to say that you could get in trouble for thinking thoughts like that but decided that would just make his point. "So you're saying politics is to blame?"

"Not entirely. Greed, ignorance and over consumption had something to do with it as well. Plus an absolute myopic refusal to admit anything was wrong until it was too late. And now we have to make the best of it."

"Do you really think that?"

"About the past? Absolutely. About the future? I'm less sure. Keris has lived through the kind of destruction it seems we're all headed for but she's got this insane belief that we'll all be okay somehow. If only we'd all wake up."

"So you wanted me for a second opinion?"

"Something like that."

"Well my opinion is that you should forget about the exotic Keris Edge and get back to work."

"I *am* working. There are reasons why we've got to the point we're at and I need to understand them before I make my decision."

"I understand you're not making much sense. Valentine, you're not going to do something stupid, are you?"

"That's what I'm very much trying to avoid."

She wasn't surprised to see Keris Edge lounging on a sofa in her apartment, beer in one hand, cigarette in the other. She wondered if she was more bothered by the breaking and entering or the narcotics violation. Neither, she concluded as she silently got a beer for herself from the refrigerator.

"So, Valentine's new girlfriend is the famous Rena Lalgi, master predictor."

"And Valentine's old girlfriend is the infamous Keris Edge, terrorist agitator. Not that I'm Valentine's new girlfriend."

"And not that I'm a terrorist agitator. Cheers."

Rena sat down in an armchair and looked her up and down. Without the wig she was actually quite pretty. Even relaxed she was much more alive than most of the people Rena normally met. She could see what had attracted Valentine.

"I'm surprised you managed to track me down so easily, or so quickly."

"In my line it pays to be ahead of the game. You weren't difficult to find."

"Does Valentine know you're here?"

Keris shook her head. "To tell you the truth, I half expected him to walk through the door with you. Where'd you meet him, anyway? You got him under surveillance or something?"

Rena realized that Keris had no idea who Valentine was.

"Heard he'd been keeping some unsavoury company. Figured I'd check out who."

"Well here I am. Truth is, I've wanted to meet you for a while. "

"Me?" Rena looked startled.

"Yeah, I'm intrigued. You're the best predictor in the Bureau, get it right ninety-nine times out of a hundred. You're a legend. And yet everyone around here thinks we're all on borrowed time. I don't. And you don't either, otherwise you'd never be able to do your job."

"I could have you arrested for breaking in here. Especially given who you are."

"Yes but you won't. And that's interesting as well, isn't it?" Keris walked over to the refrigerator and brought over two more beers.

"Keris, I'm not just a predictive analyst, I'm also an optimist. There is never any one inevitable course of action. There are too many uncertainties for that."

Keris dismissed that. "A 99% success rate tells me you don't believe that."

"It's only 94%, actually. But broadly you're right." Rena knew she shouldn't be talking to Keris about this, that what she said would inevitably end up on the streets as propaganda, but right then she didn't care. "The human race has been around for a long time. We're good at surviving."

"Tell that to the people in the Manchester Dome."

"You survived, didn't you?" Rena knew that was the wrong thing to say as soon as she said it. They drank in silence for a while.

"Yes, well plenty of people I knew didn't. But I get your point. And what's more, I agree with it. Oh sure the Manchester Dome may have failed, but this one's looking in pretty good shape. Sure the atmosphere outside's beginning to get a bit grim, but so long as we're tucked up tight, we'll be okay."

"So why have you been kicking up such a fuss then? Why don't you just carry out your assigned job and keep smiling like the rest of us?"

"Well partly it's because my assigned job is boring and pointless and designed to keep me just tired enough not to cause any trouble. And partly because I don't believe our survival is anything like inevitable."

Rena laughed. "So you want to save us by destroying us?"

"You got it. As long as we're controlled by the urban militia we're just passing the time until everything finally falls apart."

Rena took another swig. "It won't make any difference you know."

"The newspaper? Probably not, though it's worked in the past. Poland, last century, for instance."

"Valentine would be impressed. You know your history. But the Solidarity movement was going with the revolutionary grain and things had already started to soften in eastern Europe. Communism would have fallen anyway. Those regimes collapse under their own weight eventually. They decay inside and normal life resumes. Entropy."

"Entropy?"

"Long term everything smooths out in very predictable patterns. As a race we're aggressive, curious, bloody minded, fundamentally moral but quite selfish. It's not hard to predict how things are going to turn out when you slosh all that into the mix."

"Can you predict whether we're going to have another beer then?"

"You can't be precise short term without knowing all the variables," Rena said, walking to the fridge. "But that was an easy one."

Rena didn't notice the crowd standing on the street corner until she bumped into a man so hard he spilled his latte. Rena looked up to apologize but the man had barely noticed. He was looking up at the sky.

"What the hell is that?"

Latte man took a sip of what remained of his coffee.

"Looks like a man on a rope to me."

"Uh-huh."

"Abseiling. From the roof of the dome."

Rena was astounded. "Why?"

"I have absolutely no idea. Impressive, though."

If she peered hard, Rena could almost make out the man's face. The dome was about 500 meters high, more or less. Somehow the abseiler had managed to get up there and attach his ropes. The dome was made out of some super thick, super strong perspex, sheathed on both sides with a viscous membrane which made it very difficult to cling on to. Yet there he was, preparing to descend. He was directly above the middle of the dome.

He was wearing a superhero costume, the traditional uniform of protest. As he slid gracefully down the rope his cape was caught in the wind and made it look briefly as if

11

he was flying. Then, suddenly, a gunshot cracked and he stopped, abruptly, hanging in the air like a puppet.

The crowd sighed in unison, then started to break up.

"Shame," Rena ventured.

"Damndest thing I ever saw," added latte man.

Rena was appalled that the man had been shot. But the whole incident had left her enervated. Impossible feats and daring courage were the sort of things the regime was supposed to suppress, so seeing something so spectacular on the way to work was just a hint that Keris' time might have come after all. She hoped so.

Valentine looked gloomy as Rena entered the office. He was staring at a copy of their report on the East London riot.

"The boss didn't like it?" He tossed the paper to Rena, covered in red ink. She read it quickly. "But that's…"

"Not what happened. Right."

"No, more to the point, it's not what I said would happen," she replied. "I said the riots would keep happening until the dome's air circulation system was upgraded. And I said it was vital that we overhaul the militia's approach to policing there. I can't believe they needed to shoot those rioters."

"Shot with their own weapons, apparently. Temporary madness, caused by something in the water. All sorted now. Business as usual."

"But that's…"

"Dangerous nonsense? Sure. So I asked the boss about it. Apparently we don't get the bigger picture. He thinks that if we tell the Cabinet this was all about overzealous policing and penny pinching maintenance they're more likely to shout at the people who gave them the bad news than they are to sort out the problems, because that would be easier."

"That's never happened to me before." Rena was fuming.

"You've never openly criticized the regime before, though."

She'd written her report after Keris had left her apartment, emailing it early in the morning. Had she never submitted a report with a political edge before? "So they want me to stick to nice safe predictions. Keep clear of anything controversial." What was happening to her? Keris must have shaken her more than she'd realized. She'd been trained to couch her predictions in a politically neutral way, to convey the sense of the inevitable and to edit out any sense of blame or responsibility. Why had she forgotten her instincts? But there was something else. "Valentine, last night?"

"Yes?"

"You were about to tell me something. About a choice you had to make."

Valentine grabbed his jacket. "Let's walk."

Valentine led them to the southwestern edge of the dome. Rena could see the old Chelsea Bridge lying, battered, beyond the perimeter. "I was born over there, in the old Chelsea hospital. Not much left now." He looked sheepish. "Nothing here for me anymore. Time to move on, don't you think?"

Rena looked at him. He was carrying himself differently, as though he had new purpose. He went on. "I've been offered a place on the third Explorer mission. The third escape craft."

Suddenly Rena knew what he wanted from Keris. And from her. He wanted them to talk him out of it.

"It's all hopeless," he continued. "And the authorities are in denial. You saw that today. The East London Dome is finished. And after that, where next? How long before the riots start here too?"

"That's not going to happen, Valentine."

"Is that a prediction?"

She ignored the question. "Which mission is it?"

13

"Third ship's going to 51 Pegasus."

She frowned. "Do you know what you're going to find when you wake up—*if* you wake up—in a hundred years? A planet that's slightly too close to its sun to be comfortable, full of active volcanoes and violent weather events. You should feel right at home."

"At least I'll be free."

"Will you? Free to do what, exactly?"

"Free to expand. Free to grow. Free from this sense of defeatism everyone round here seems to have."

Rena looked round at the devastation beyond the barrier. It had a grey infectiousness about it, an encroaching sense of dread and foreboding. She could see why people clustered in the middle of the domes, away from the ominous portents at the edge. It was a vision of hell, and a reminder that damnation was just around the corner. If you believed in the inevitable onrushing of the night, she reminded herself.

"Valentine, you trust me, don't you? And you know I'm usually right about the way things are going to turn out. Well I agree with Keris. We're too resilient for all this. It's our job to keep things together until it gets better. And it will."

"In our lifetimes?"

"It doesn't matter when it happens. It just matters that it's going to."

"And if it doesn't?"

"Then we aren't the stubborn, cussed survivors I think we are. The trouble with you, Valentine, is that your predictions are all wrong. You're so used to looking at things after the event that you see potential disaster in everything. You see a bomb, you predict an explosion. You see disaster happening in one badly built dome the other side of London, you predict it's going to happen here. It's no wonder you're a pessimist." They began to walk back along the embankment. "When do you have to make your decision?"

"Next week. Ship leaves the week after."

"I can't believe you're even contemplating this. You get travel sick on the top floor of the bus, so how you'll cope with 50 light years is a complete mystery."

"I'll be asleep, don't forget."

"You'd better hope so."

They met later that evening in a pub round the corner from Blackfriars Station, another old Victorian with low ceilings and oak panels and real, working gas lanterns. Valentine hadn't argued when Rena insisted on coming. Rena hadn't told him about Keris' visit. Keris embraced her warmly.

"Something I missed?"

"Later, Valentine," said Keris "Let's just say she's more than welcome here."

Evans and Price showed up, with beers. The bar was crowded, but they managed to squeeze in to a table. Over the next two hours Keris sketched out her plan, which, basically, was to break in to the TV station and replace the usual programming with some alternative footage of their own. Rena knew that Keris probably had the skills to do that remotely, but where was the dramatic flair in that?

The next day was a Saturday and Rena got up late. If things had gone according to plan there should be something on the TV and that something should be Keris. Rena scratched her head as she shuffled into the kitchen for some coffee. The TV was showing the usual stuff. Perhaps she was early. She checked her watch. Actually, she was late. That meant the plan hadn't worked.

It was late afternoon before her phone rang. It was Keris.

"Apparently I get one call and you're it."

"You're in jail?"

"Militia station. Bet you didn't predict that one."

"What happened?"

"Later, later. Just get down here, okay?"

#

15

Keris sat glumly on a hard plastic chair in a holding cell, hands cuffed. She clearly hadn't slept.

"You okay?"

"Been better. Good to see you, though."

"Want to talk about it?"

Keris' cockiness had evaporated. "Militia bashed the door in about two o'clock."

"What do they know?"

"Just about everything. They knew about the TV station plot, knew about the newspaper. Didn't know about you and Valentine, though. That's why it's good to see you. Had to be you or Valentine, I figured. Glad it wasn't you."

Keris was in line for some public humiliation, and she knew it. Rena dashed from the militia building in a hurry. She had to find Valentine, find out what he'd done. Find out why. It was deep into the evening before she tracked him down, staring out over the ruins of Chelsea Bridge watching the crimson sun sink below the jagged remains of the West London skyline.

"Have you got anything to say for yourself, Valentine?"

Valentine turned. She could see he'd been crying. "I wasn't entirely straight with you before, Rena. About the escape flight. Didn't you stop to wonder why they'd offered me a place on the ship?"

Everything had always come so easily to Valentine that she'd simply assumed that that sort of offer was commonplace to him.

"I had to trade, Rena. I had to trade Keris."

Rena stared at Valentine, too shocked to speak.

"Don't you see?" he went on. "We have to survive. I have to survive. I have to go."

"And Keris?"

"I had to choose."

She looked at him closely for the last time.

"Well I sincerely hope it was worth it."

She turned away. There was no more to be said.

#

She didn't see him again. Not in the flesh. But she saw the launch on TV. He was back to his old handsome self on the news shots, the old swagger back, the tears gone.

Valentine had cut a better deal with the authorities than he might have. He'd presented Keris as an unwitting dupe in the whole operation, laying most of the blame on Evans and Price. And he'd made it clear that she was to be let off lightly. He was one of the most photogenic of the new astronauts and the authorities badly needed his continued co-operation. So Keris got let off with a stiff fine and a stern warning, providing she could get a responsible citizen to vouch for her. So that's how she ended up at Rena's place.

Two years later they set off on their great expedition. They left the dome in a heavily armoured secure vehicle and headed to Portsmouth, to the nuclear submarine still moored there. Rena had official sanction for this trip: she had predicted a need for some first-hand information on what was going on in the rest of the world and had risen sufficiently highly in the Bureau to make the whole trip happen. No one in her group had ever piloted a submarine before but they had the manuals and they had the enthusiasm.

And more importantly, they had hope.

The Beggar and the Golden Dome

Worst case scenario, the scientists said, back in old, more optimistic times. Now London's domes stood gleaming and serene while all around them the world decayed, battered by the new extremities of an increasingly hostile climate. Inside the domes life went on, much as it had before. Outside? You wouldn't want to be outside.

Jake shivered, pulled his threadbare coat tight and shuffled disconsolately through the rubble.

Anna put a hand gently on his shoulder. "Come on. We need to get under shelter."

Exposure to the harshness of the post-collapse climate had left her skin dry and taut and cracked at the mouth. She hunched slightly, hair unkempt and fraying. She was thirty but looked fifty. Jake realised he must look like that, too.

Anna went first down the narrow, steep steps into the deep basement; all that remained of the old house they had been squatting in. Once, he imagined, it stood proud in its leafy Notting Hill street. Now it was flattened, like the rest of the city.

The others were hard at work. Max repairing something mechanical in the corner, lost in his own thoughts. Dawn cooking over the open fire: soup, by the smell of it. Max glanced up. Jake could see the hopeful look on his face fade as he caught Jake's expression. "Sorry, Max. We went as far as Acton. We found nothing."

Max nodded and went back to his work. "Then you'll need to go further tomorrow."

"Max, I don't think you've been listening. We've finally run out. Everywhere. London's a big place but it's not that big. We aren't the only people trying to eat, you know."

As if on cue Dawn said "Soup's ready," and they all sat round the makeshift table to eat. It was thin stuff. The cupboard was nearly bare.

"Good soup." Jake said, as much to break the silence as to make conversation.

Dawn smiled. "Thanks. There's more in the pot. If we're careful it should last us for a couple of days."

They finished. Jake went over to his coat, hanging on a hook by the door. He rummaged in a pocket and brought out four chocolate bars and threw them on the table with a flourish.

"Jake! Have you been holding out?" Anna said.

Jake grinned. "I found them under a bed in that big house we searched. Maybe someone kept them for midnight snacks."

Dawn ripped off the wrapping on her bar and crammed it into her mouth. She spoke through noisy chews. "Bad for you, chocolate, Got any more?"

"You found a house, standing?" Max said, suddenly alert.

"Yeah. Three of them, actually. We came across them in Shepherds Bush, protected by a high wall and in a bit of a dip. They're solidly built Georgian things. Squat, so there's not much to fall over. The firestorm must have passed them by."

"Habitable?"

"Um. Yes. No chocolate left, though. Max, what's got you so excited?"

Max looked at him as though he was stupid. "Jake, have you looked at this place?"

Jake shrugged. To humour Max he looked around. The place was untidy, as usual, but it looked quite pleasant in the candlelight, homely even with the warm glow from the fire crackling in the large open fireplace. Apart from the puddles. He couldn't remember seeing any puddles before. "Where's the water coming from?" he asked.

Dawn sighed. "It's the rain, Jake. Never stops."

"But we're watertight. We made sure of that when we moved in."

Max sat down again and leaned forward. He had a manic look in his eyes. "Yes but that was two years ago. Since then it's done nothing but rain. Which means the ground is saturated. The water isn't coming down through the roof, it's coming up from the ground."

"But we're on high ground."

"We're not that high, not any more, not now the river's spread. Anyway, it doesn't matter. The water table under London was shot even in the old days. When the tube actually worked they used to pump out millions of gallons a day, just to keep it from flooding.

"Now that there's no-one using it, and all this rain filling it up, the level keeps on rising. I reckon we've got a week, maybe two, before this basement fills up permanently."

Jake and Anna looked at each other, scared.

"Hence my interest in the big house you found," Max went on.

Jake shook his head. "Won't work. Those houses are standing out like rotten teeth now. Next big storm and they'll be gone too. And there's still no food."

Dawn began to rock gently in her seat. Anna scowled.

"We have to leave, don't we?" Anna said, calmly,

Max just nodded. Jake pushed his seat back and stood up.

"Tomorrow. We'll head right out to the countryside, No-one's going anywhere tonight."

They set off just after dawn, inching though the wreckage of the city carefully, skirting round any obvious hazards and keeping well clear of any fallen buildings. The rain had stopped, and though the air was still and cold it had an early morning crispness that held the promise it would turn into a warm day. For that Jake was grateful. It was July and the days were supposed to be warm.

21

Jake led them though the ruins of Holland Park and down to the old A40 route out of London. The roadway was wide and smooth and the path significantly clearer than the narrow streets closer to the centre of town. Rubble had still spread from the surrounding streets, though, and every now and then a big jagged rent checked their progress and made them detour. But it was a pathway which they all knew led out of town. Such an obvious route, though, made Jake feel uneasy.

By the time they got to the North Circular the sun was high in the sky. Apart from a solitary cat, which had scurried away as soon as it had seen them, they'd seen nothing else alive since they started out.

They sat on what used to be a garden wall. The garden, and the house which stood in it, were mostly gone. Dawn unpacked her rucksack and brought out forks and some food. A tin of baked beans each, hoarded many months before.

"It's spooky, isn't it. There used to be millions of people living here. Now these streets are empty." Dawn took a last scoop from her can.

"Oh there are people still here, all right," said Jake. "Hiding, just like we were. Waiting for whatever final humiliation the weather's got in store for us. Anna and I see traces of them sometimes, when we're scavenging. Warm fires, piles of empty cans. I even saw a kid once, not so long ago. Ran when I called out to him. Ran and vanished."

"How many people do you think are left, Jake?" asked Max.

"Out here? Not enough. In there?" He gestured back at the Westminster Dome, still visible on the horizon. "Too many." There were six, all strung together, from the East End to the West, together holding a couple of hundred thousand people at most. Refuges from the apocalypse.

"They have room for us." Anna said. "We should make them take us."

Jake knew Anna resented the dome people for keeping them out but he thought he understood their inhumanity, just a little. They were selfish and they were scared. But that didn't give them an excuse to abandon the dwindling band of survivors outside.

"We have to keep moving," said Max. "We've got miles to go yet before we hit the edge of town. And we need to find a secure shelter before nightfall."

They kept walking until they could walk no more. At least it had stopped raining, Jake thought miserably as they shuffled in the twilight. But with the dark came the familiar chilling cries of wild dogs, and the group fell still.

"I can't go on." Dawn's voice was a quiet, defeated murmur.

"Nor me," echoed Anna. Max just shrugged.

"Here, then." Jake pointed to the wreck of a bus, lying on its side across the carriageway. "Tonight's hotel."

The bus was gutted. But lying on its back its roof and undercarriage became sidewalls, and that meant protection. It was open to the sky, and that meant if it rained they were likely to get wet. But they could keep the dogs out, and they would be safe.

They slept, fitfully, and emerged in the dawn light tired and hungry. "We were lucky," said Jake to no-one in particular. "It didn't rain."

"This is the last time we'll have to do this," said Max, sniffing the air. "Proper shelter tonight."

"Dream on," said Jake, turning his back. Anna passed him his tattered bag and they set off down the road.

"Don't say it," Anna touched Jake gently on the arm. By mid-afternoon they had just crossed the point at which the M40 crosses the M25. The point at which Jake had always thought the city ends and the countryside begins. But this was a strange, desolate countryside filled with ruined buildings and dark, anaemic looking vegetation.

23

Max said it instead. "Too wet. The ground's swamped. It won't be easy to grow crops here."

They reached an old farmhouse, shielded from the wind by the contours of a small hill. Max kicked down the door. Two young girls huddled in the bedroom, wrapped in blankets and shivering. In their wasted state Jake had no idea how old they were. Both the girls flinched when Anna approached them. Neither responded when Max asked them who they were, or where their parents were.

"They're in shock, Max," Jake pulled his friend back. "If they had parents they wouldn't be here, like this, would they?"

Max nodded, conceding the point. With some coaxing, Anna and Dawn managed to persuade the girls to come with them. They didn't talk much, but what they did say confirmed Jake's fears.

"Where's your mum and dad?" said Anna to the oldest girl.

"Mum's dead. She got sick when the food ran out. Dad? Dunno. He didn't come back one day. Raiders got him."

"Raiders?"

"We hid in the cellar and they went away."

Jake could see no sign of the raiders now, but he stayed wary. Heathrow Airport was close by so they headed there, because they couldn't think of anything else to do. There were still some planes on the tarmac, though most of them were broken and crushed by the incessant wind and storms which whipped ferociously down the Thames Valley.

They ate the last of their food that night in the one and only hangar still standing. Jake reckoned it must have been open when the first storms hit, with the doors facing the direction of the wind. He couldn't think of any other reason it would still be there. The terminal buildings were crushed and shattered, but there were vending machines in the wreckage, and tonight they were dining on chocolate.

During the night the youngest girl died.

"You know this isn't going to work," said Jake, morosely, as they wrapped the body in an old sheet they'd found in the corner of the hangar. The other girl slept as Dawn gently stroked her hair

"We press on," said Max.

"No, we go back."

"We can't, not now." said Anna. "Just us and I'd agree. But we've got the girl to think about. She's called Cassie. She's ten. And she'll die for sure if we take her back to the city. We all will."

After they buried Cassie's sister and gathered up their few belongings the others started to move off. Jake hung back. When Anna got to the hangar door she turned and retraced her steps.

"You're not coming, are you?" she said.

"I don't want to bury Cassie as well. Bad enough we had to bury her sister." Jake couldn't look at her.

"She was called Anna, like me."

"I don't want to know her name. Names are for the living."

"We need you."

"No. You have Max. He believes you can make it out there. I know you can't."

Anna looked about to argue but seemed to think better of it. "You'll go back?"

"To the dome. There's nowhere else to go."

And so he left, and he was alone.

It was still there, as he'd remembered it, serene and majestic. He hadn't been that close to the dome for many years, and he kept a respectful distance to avoid alerting the guards, resting behind a low jagged wall and peering out only occasionally.

He wanted to just sit there and watch, but he was too hungry and he knew he needed to find a way in quickly. It was opaque, and if there had been any sun in the sky its surface would have been a dazzling mirror. Now it just gave off a slightly golden glow. He could see nothing of its interior, but he'd dreamed of its wide avenues and timeless buildings many times.

He must have slept, because when he opened his eyes it was night. And someone was shining a torch in his face.

"This one's nearly dead already. Not worth the bullet."

Jake shielded his eyes. "You're from the Dome?"

The two men ignored him. At least Jake thought they were both men. With the blinding light of the torch beam in his eyes he could barely make out their silhouettes. But the one who had talked was definitely male. He heard a pistol cock.

"No," said the other one. He was wrong. Definitely a woman.

"Look Rena," the man turned to speak to her and Jake could see again, "this is what we do, okay?"

They were dressed in black padded suits, like the kind the police used to wear to deal with riots. They were wearing tight fitting black helmets which shielded their faces.

The man carried on talking. He sounded exasperated. "They all want to get in, right? And they can't, because there's not enough room for them. And they've all got diseases."

"This one looks healthy enough. Half starved, maybe, but he doesn't look sick."

"You want to take a chance? Besides, living out here they get sick in the head. What do you think they live on, eh? When they can't find any rats to chew on?"

"That's ridiculous."

It wasn't, and Jake had learned to steer clear of South London because of the rumours that it was a one-way trip for the unwary. That and the severed heads hanging from burnt out traffic lights. But there were plenty of rats, if you knew where to find them. Without them Jake, Anna and the others would have been a long time dead.

"We let this one in, then tomorrow there'll be ten thousand of them. Beggars, draining us dry. What do we do then, eh?"

"There has to be a better way than this."

"Believe me, Rena, there isn't. Besides, I've got orders."

"What, to go out and kill people in the name of humanity? What does that do to _your_ humanity, Prentiss?" She poked a finger at his chest. Prentiss jabbed back.

"Don't lecture me. You wanted to see what we have to do to keep the dome all safe and snug so you can sit in your fancy air conditioned office and eat your three meals a day – well now you know."

They were completely engrossed in their argument. Jake knew he wouldn't have a better opportunity. He began to crawl, and before long he'd edged out of sight.

"Where's he gone?"

From his hiding place in the gap under a pile of rubble Jake couldn't see them, but he knew where they were. Close, but not close enough. Jack could hear Prentiss running around, trying to see where he'd escaped to.

"Damn it Rena. He's got away. He'll be miles away by now."

"Are you going to track him down?"

"What, and get even more grief from you? Let the regular patrols get him. We're going back."

Jake waited until the sounds of their argument began to quieten before following, taking care not to be seen. They reached a grille embedded in the ground on an old decaying piece of roadway, not much larger than a manhole cover. Prentiss pointed a device and it opened slowly.

Jake was on him before he had time to react, pushing him to the floor. In one easy, fluid movement, Jake pulled the gun from the holster on Prentiss's hip and held it tightly to his neck. Rena, looking startled, backed away.

"Don't say anything. When I let you go, undress. Throw your clothes over there."

Jake couldn't hide his contempt as Prentiss slowly stripped down to his underwear. Naked and shivering, he looked defiantly at Jake. "You going to eat me now, scum? See Rena? Told you what they were like."

Rena still hadn't moved. Jake kept his eye on her but she seemed to be frozen in panic. "Take your helmet off," he said.

She did it slowly, revealing a long angular face with high cheekbones and piercing blue eyes. Well fed, he noticed, with long hair tied back, clean and shining. He hadn't seen freshly washed hair for quite some time. He looked straight into her eyes gauging her expression. He'd anticipated fear, but what he saw was more like expectation. He hoped he was about to make the right decision.

"You can't kill him," she said.

"I'm not going to kill him. Hold this. Point it at him. I need to get changed." Jake passed her the gun.

She grabbed it and, hesitating for just a second, pointed it at Prentiss.

"Rena, what the hell are you doing?" Prentiss started to take a step forward, stopping when he heard the distinctive click of the safety catch.

"Not another step," said Rena, as Jake started to put on Prentiss's clothes. When he finished he clicked his helmet visor down. Now he looked just like Prentiss had. He threw his rags over. Prentiss stared at them, visibly trembling. Jake took the gun back from Rena and waited until Prentiss had finished dressing. Then he waved vaguely at the ruins in the distance.

"Keep low and watch out for the dogs. Make sure you only drink fresh rainwater and check it's not contaminated. And if you're going to eat rats, cook them first."

"That all you've got to say?"

"Head West. The people are friendly out there. Mostly. Now run. Or do I have to shoot?"

Prentiss slunk away. Jake kept his gun trained until he could no longer see him.

"Will he be all right out there?" Rena asked.

Jake shrugged. "Depends what you mean by 'all right'. He can survive, if he wants to, and he can stay out of trouble. No doubt you people will let him back in before he comes to too much harm."

Jake followed her through the grille and into a long, poorly lit passageway. The opening closed behind them and they passed quickly along, moving in the direction of the dome.

"How did you know?" asked Rena. "That you could trust me, I mean."

"I didn't. Not completely. But sometimes you have to go with your gut. And I knew I couldn't get in without you so I had to take the chance."

"Okay so you guessed I wouldn't let Prentiss kill you. You got lucky. But why should I help you now?"

"Because you've pulled a gun on Prentiss and now you're committed. And because we both know if you make me go back I'll die out there. And unless you were lying out there to Prentiss, I don't think you could live with that."

They reached a thick metal door secured with a large round handle, like the ones Jake had seen in submarine movies. Rena took off her left glove and placed her bare hand against a pad next to the door. It began to slide open.

"You presume a lot." Rena looked at him coldly.

"I'm Jake, by the way. And I'm very grateful."

Rena slid through the doorway. Jake followed. They were in a brightly lit chamber with another metal door at the far end.

"Don't take your helmet off. When we get through, keep your head down and walk as far and as casually as you can until you're absolutely certain no one is looking at you and no one has followed you. Then lose those clothes. Then lose yourself."

"They'll kill me if they catch me."

She hesitated, then nodded. "Then we'd better make sure they don't catch you."

Out in the light Jake looked up at the buildings, intact and proud. Mature trees lined the avenues, achingly alive with a green vibrancy which made him wish he could take off his helmet and breathe deeply, to envelop himself in their long-remembered scent. There were people everywhere, clearly well fed and well clothed in clean, gaudy fabrics, hurrying to wherever they were going with their heads down in determined scowls. It was as if the last twenty years had not happened.

They took a bright yellow electric taxi to her apartment, on the top floor of a low-rise thirties block of ex-housing association properties behind Victoria Street. A policeman in riot clothing similar to Jake's nodded at him, rifle raised. Jake waved back and tried not to choke on his fear. He hardly noticed that the communal areas were strewn with rubbish. His eyes were more drawn to the thick metal high security door guarding Rena's apartment. The paintwork was scuffed and faded and there was clear evidence of a break in attempt, though it didn't look recent. He glanced around and saw twin CCTV cameras embedded in the corridors. To his relief, the interior of the flat looked freshly painted, clean and tidy. And safe.

"There's food in the fridge. Stay here until I come back. And don't do anything stupid."

He was watching TV when she returned, old reruns of an ancient American cop drama. He guessed they weren't making any new stuff. She threw a bundle of papers at him.

"Jake, right? Just come down from the Manchester Dome. How's your accent?"

"How did you get these?" Jake was impressed.

"I'm connected. And like you said, I'm committed. We have to make this work."

"But if Prentiss comes back?"

"Let's hope he doesn't."

One year later, and with his well-developed sense of irony still intact, Jake pulled his patrolman's jacket tightly around him and scanned the wasteland for signs of life. Since the riots in the East London Dome had drawn away half their firepower they were running one man patrols and today Jake was following up on some movement the remote drones had detected near the ruins of the old Chelsea Bridge.

They appeared right in front of him. He hardly recognised them at first. An emaciated old woman, with half her hair gone, clutching a small child tightly by the hand. The child looked miserable, and Jake could see the beginnings of malnutrition distorting her features and distending her belly. She looked about six or seven years old. Jake remembered her name was Cassie and the last time he saw her she was ten.

"Help us. I'm begging you."

Jake lifted his visor. "Hello, Anna."

He should have shot her. He should have shot all of them, but that's not why he took the job.

"Max and the others?"

Anna shook her head and stared at the floor. Jake could see the blisters on her skin clearly.

"I'm sorry." Jake reached out his arms to her.

"Don't be. Just don't say 'I told you so', okay?"

Before Anna there had been a slow trickle of refugees from the poisoned, blackened countryside. He'd managed to save a few, hoping they weren't carrying any infectious diseases. He'd been careful, making them think that they'd escaped from him and found the open grating all by themselves. At first he knew they were people like him, desperate for a chance to survive. Later, though, all he could see was the cold needy hatred in their eyes. Until Anna, he'd not opened his visor to any of them.

Anna and the child were the last survivors Jake saw. He sometimes heard howling in the distance and though he liked to think it was the sound of wild dogs, deep in his heart he knew it wasn't. The landscape - and the people - out there had transformed and he was vaguely aware he was changing himself. He knew with a certain terrifying resolve that the next time he saw beggars outside the golden dome he wouldn't lead them to safety. He would see the feral glint in their eyes, recoil from the boils and blisters pockmarking their thin and tattered bodies and reach for his pistol.

For Hannah

Three days in space and it doesn't seem like a good idea anymore. I've been vomiting almost constantly, and I think the Captain would throw me out of the airlock if she could. I'd even help her open the hatches. I should be back in my workshop developing software instead of lying in a tiny bunk in a cramped cabin wondering how I'm going to make it through the rest of the day. Our ship, the *Celestial Paragon,* is bound for Erasmus, third planet out from 61 Virginis, and that's going to take us almost twelve years. But because time does funny things when you go really fast, it'll seem quicker on the ship than on the planet. So at ship velocity, nudging the speed of light, almost thirty years will have passed on Erasmus by the time we get there. Hannah will be seventy-four years old. And I'll be forty-three.

We're weightless at the moment, in orbit, waiting for the engineers to do their final checks on the engine so we can be on our way. I keep telling myself that the nausea will pass once we're finally moving and the ship's artificial gravity kicks in. Enjoy it while it lasts, said the Captain. The main cargo deck has been turned into some sort of freefall pleasure room where those with stronger stomachs can entertain themselves. I'm not intending to leave my cabin.

Hannah smiles at me from the chair. She looks concerned and leans towards me. She stretches out, as if to touch my shoulder, but of course she can't. She's got her hair tied back today, all business like and ready, because this is a big day for her, too.

"Jim," she says. "I'm afraid."

"I'm doing this for you. So we can be together. Properly."

She leans back and crosses her arms. Even when she's angry she's beautiful. Brown hair, tiny frame, freckles, dimples, dressed in an olive jump suit that should be baggy but somehow seems to add definition. She looks away, out towards the porthole window that gazes out over the starry blackness. I follow her eyes. I can just see Earth's rim peeking over the bottom edge of the window. It makes me feel dizzy and I grab hold of the bed frame for support. Then I rush to the bathroom. When I return, she is gone.

She doesn't reappear until we're properly under way. She's not scowling anymore, though I can't say she looks happy. Wistful, maybe. She has her hair cut short today, in a style that doesn't really suit her. I don't mind. "You're not mad at me?" I say, though I know she is.

"Nothing I can do about it, is there? We're on our way now." I see she's been picking at her fingernails. I don't understand how she can do that, why her algorithms include nervous habits like that. But I don't really understand where she goes when she dematerialises. I know she doesn't always go to the virtual world we built, that sometimes she breaks through the coding and ends up somewhere else. She tells me every time I ask but all her explanations are slightly different and it's easier just to think she simply isn't here when she's not with me.

I'm with Hannah because I have a lot of money and she's not real. And because I know how to design things. And because she's the only woman I ever fell in love with.

"Nobody on Earth is good enough for you," said my last girlfriend, just before she roared off in my new Aston. She was right.

"You should have stuck with an avatar," says Hannah, as if reading my thoughts. "Then you wouldn't be making this trip."

But I know the woman I love has to be more than just a construction. An avatar wouldn't be real. I couldn't trust her love for me."

"And you trust mine? Hannah – the real Hannah – is on Erasmus. I'm just a data stream. And it's not as if I'm in a position to date anyone else."

"Do you love me?"

"Yes, dammit."

"There you are, then."

She looks exasperated. "That's not an answer."

But it's all I have.

I remember the first day I discovered that Hannah was out there. She was the daughter of the first community leader in Jefferson, which was what the first settlers had named their capital city. It's not the capital now, of course. That's Hanoi, or at least it was twelve years ago.

We sent the very best communications technicians out there, and the very best equipment. So it wasn't surprising that the feed from Erasmus was clear and sharp, capable of sending exabytes of information every second. And that's enough for a whole human being, stripped back into digital form, including a comprehensive brain map.

They wanted our scientists to see what effect prolonged spaceflight had on the human body, and the human mind, so they sent a copy of Hannah through, right down to her annoying nail biting habit. They sent her just before they landed. She was just seventeen.

Then five years later they sent her again, just so we could see the effect Erasmus would have on her. By that time I'd turned Phoenix Systems into the world leader in virtual environments, and I was the one they turned to when the realised they'd get more from Hannah by talking to her than by taking her apart byte by byte.

She never had a real body, of course. That wasn't my field. There was talk of one, eventually, but the science wasn't there yet. They wanted to grow one – actually grow a clone from the DNA they had stored – so they could stick Hannah's mind in once it had reached adulthood, but an ethical argument raged about the clone's right to live, and that meant they never really got started.

So I had no choice really, not when I started to fall in love.

I created a virtual environment for her to live in, and a holographic interface so that she could communicate with the outside world. With me.

At first she was in much demand, initially with scientists, then with the media. She gave speeches, appeared on talk shows, watched patiently whilst the President sipped tea in the Oval Office and told her how astonishing she was.

Then the media lost interest, and the scientists stopped doing their tests, and then it was just me. Well. Me and the virtual world I built for her, modelled on Erasmus and her memories.

We made love for the first time on V-Erasmus. Afterwards, as we lay on the river bank in the deepening twilight, with the boxy grey architecture of Jefferson shining in the distance, I turned to her and knew what I needed to do.

Captain Hendricks looks amused, but I can't tell if she's laughing at me or with me. Hannah's away in V-Erasmus, or at least the stripped down version of it that's possible with my portable array. I conclude that Hendricks is laughing at me.

"What if she doesn't want you?" She's talking through a mouthful of food and prodding at me with her chopsticks. I look at the noodles in my own bowl and push them away up the table.

"Why wouldn't she? They're the same. My Hannah loves me. The other one will as well."

"You really don't know women, do you?" She takes a long slurp of her cola, even though she still has rice in her mouth. She burps. "One, since you're not around, the real Hannah will have found someone else."

"Ah, but she won't be happy. Not without me."

"You're delusional. But you've paid for your passage and I like you. You make me laugh. You finished with that?" She looks down at my discarded bowl and adds the noodles to her pile. "Two," she continues, "she won't even be like your Hannah. She'll be older. How do you even know what your Hannah's going to turn out like?"

I smile. "My company specialises in extrapolation programmes – growth, if you like. We can determine the causal and genetic factors which make someone what they are, then work out how they'll be when they're older. Our techniques are in demand with law enforcement agencies around the world because we can tell them who the criminals are, even if they haven't committed a crime yet. You heard the expression 'it's in the genes'? Well that's partly right, and we know how to work out the rest."

"So that's how you got so damn rich."

I can feel my cheeks reddening. "Most people aren't so rude to me."

"Most people are probably impressed by your money, which, incidentally, won't buy you diddly squat on my ship. Me? I'm the Captain, you're the passenger. I've got two hundred others just like you and you're sitting here eating at my table not because you paid for the whole damn trip, but because you are very entertaining. So entertain me some more."

I tell her about the experiment we did with the first Hannah data stream, the one we got when she was seventeen, and extrapolated what she might be like when she was twenty three, the age my Hannah was when she first arrived back on Earth. Even I was surprised at how minimal the differences were. After that it was even easier because we had two time points to triangulate against. That way we could see not just how Hannah would grow but how her environment would develop as well. I built that information into her algorithms, so that Hannah could grow with me. I even knew what she would be like when she was seventy-four.

"Same time tomorrow, Asher?" she says, as she piles up both our bowls and heads for the kitchen area.

So I am friends with the Captain. That makes me smile.

Hannah isn't amused. "How can I compete with her? She's flesh and blood."

"She's too large. She eats too much. And she's rude to me."

"I'm rude to you. That's one of the things you said you like about me."

There's so much more to my love for Hannah, and she knows it. So instead of carrying on the argument, I search for my immersion headset. "We could take a walk by the stream. We haven't done that for a while. And," I smile, "that's something Captain Hendricks will never be able to do."

"Until we get to Erasmus, you mean." But she drops the subject, and I drop into her world. We are not, as I expected, by the stream but in the main square outside a café. A man at a table nearby is talking too loudly and blowing cigar smoke towards me. I steer us away.

It's noisy. I don't remember the background hum, the steady throb of traffic and machinery. It's busier than I remember too. People in business suits are walking swiftly across the square in all directions. At each corner is a large tower, full of offices.

"It's different," I say as I glare at a glass triangular sculpture in the middle of the square.

Hannah laughs. "You only want to visit the lake."

"Why did you bring me here then?"

"Maybe I don't want to visit the lake anymore."

I sniff the air. It feels wrong, somehow. The mix is different in Erasmus anyway, but it's not that. Nor is it the gravity modifiers, which used to be set at 90% Earth norm, to simulate Erasmus' weaker pull, but which I'd had to sacrifice to save power. I hadn't realised just how much had changed in moving Hannah's virtual world onto the ship. I still have access to a staggering amount of computing power, but nothing compared to the massive linked array I had back on Earth. It's all there of course, just that the colours are off, somehow, and the sharpness in places is a little bit too sharp. Hannah, though, is just as she was. Most of my computing power devotes itself to keeping her that way.

She asked me once, when I was planning this, whether she'd age aboard the ship, the way she did back on Earth. "It's in your matrix," I replied. "Of course you'll age. You'll respond to the experiences around you. And don't forget, you've made this trip before. We know how you'll react." But that was a lie, and I think she knew it. I couldn't afford the computing power. She would grow, but not in ways I could predict any more. And she wouldn't look any older than she does today. I hold her hand and we walk to a café across the square. There are no loud men with cigars, so we sit.

"What will Erasmus be like when we get there?" she asks.

I wave away the waiter but Hannah calls him back and orders a bottle of water. It gives me time to think about my reply. "It'll be twelve years before we arrive. And we're already twelve years behind in real-time, because your memories travelled twelve years to get to us."

"Twenty four, then."

"Plus the time dilation. That adds another twenty five."

She counts on her fingers, then slips her hand back in mine. "Forty nine years from now."

"Fewer for us."

"So much will have changed."

"We predict a war. If we could teleport there, right now, we'd probably find ourselves in the middle of it."

The waiter arrives with her water bottle. She sips. "What caused it?"

I shrug. "Stupidity, like it always does. Specifically, though, the economy collapsed, like it always does. Apparently there are some racial tensions, too."

"Do you know which side wins?"

"No side wins a war. But I'm confident you'll be fit and well when we arrive."

She stares out into the square and drops her hand from mine. "You mean she will."

I ignore her. "You'll probably even look young, too. Your scientists were making considerable progress in regeneration techniques when your last data stream came through." Our software had suggested a considerable margin for error on that prediction, unusually, but I don't mention that.

I order a coffee. It's supposed to taste like the real thing. That's one of our big sales points, back at Phoenix. Eat, drink, the sensation's just like it would be back in the real world. You'll even get drunk, if you drink too much. If you want to. But this stuff tastes like tar and has an unpleasant smell. I tell Hannah that I want to go back.

"As you wish," she says, and takes another mouthful of water. "I think I'll stay."

I take my headset off and realise I'm sweating.

One day I find her sitting in the restaurant talking to the Captain. I am momentarily confused, then I realise she has managed to communicate with the ship's AI and is making use of the restaurant's holo-projectors. I had mentioned the possibility earlier to her. I hadn't realised she would be able to make that happen without me, though. I feel unbalanced.

She turns to me and smiles. "I'm not worried about you flirting with the Captain anymore."

"You're not my type," says Hendricks. She winks at Hannah. I stare at them both for a moment then turn away.

"I'm going to show Caz round Erasmus. If you don't mind."

I hadn't known the Captain's first name. Not such good friends then. "Why should I?" I say, and look away. "You could show her the stream." I go to the kitchen to prepare myself some food. When I return they are gone.

We are six months from Earth now, and the sun has dropped back into the mass of stars in our wake. Ahead, 61 Virginis is growing, but it is still a speck. I find it difficult to think of as home, but of course, when we reach our destination, no other star will ever warm me. I shiver at the thought, and wonder what is happening back on Earth. But, I try to tell myself, I haven't left my old life behind but brought it with me, because there is no-one but Hannah. But something has changed.

I want to eat in my room, but Hendricks insists I join her in the Captain's private dining quarters. I didn't even know she had a private dining room, since she always ate with the crew and passengers. I half expect Hannah to be there, too, but the table is set for two. She gestures me to sit, then follows. The table is set formally, with china and linen, and what looks like real silver cutlery. One of the kitchen staff, in formal whites, waits by the door. Hendricks nods to him, and he leaves the room.

"She's beautiful," says Hendricks and at first I think she's talking about Hannah.

"Yes. She is."

"I never imagined." She leans forwards. "So much like Earth, but so much more."

Ah. Erasmus. I relax.

She continues. "They haven't even scratched the surface of what that place is capable of, with that ridiculous city of theirs. Did you see the forest? Those trees are astounding. And those little lizard like things that look up at you with those big green eyes?

"What did you do?" I almost don't want to hear the answer.

"Talked to Hannah's boss. Borrowed a plane. Did some sightseeing. Flew over the largest waterfall I ever saw. Saw dinosaurs too, bigger than anything that ever lived on Earth. I guess that's because of the lower gravity."

I carefully fold my napkin, then look up to see if the captain is joking. "Hannah doesn't have a boss, of course."

"Sure she does. You do know she works for a logistics company, shipping stuff between Jefferson and the Outer Cities?"

I try to recover my composure. "Of course."

Hendricks laughs. I wonder when our food will arrive so I can change the subject. "Only it sounds like you didn't. What do you think she does all day? Wander around? She's got to eat, you know. And the way you've got her programmed, she's got to do it in that virtual world of yours. So yes, she's got a job. A good one, which pays enough for that fancy apartment of hers."

My collar is too tight. I loosen it. "You saw her apartment?"

She laughs again. "Don't worry – I didn't go anywhere near the bedroom. And she's not my type either. Turns out she's in love with someone else."

I surprise myself by asking the question. "Me?"

She surprises me by not replying. Then the food arrives and we talk about the duty roster.

We may be passengers but we all have jobs to do. Three hours a day, the psychologist advised, is enough to stave off complete boredom. My job is entertainment co-ordinator, and the idea is that at least once a week we bring the entire ship's complement together for communal activities, designed to strengthen team bonding. I've devised a number of virtual scenarios that I hope will cause everyone to bond so tightly that after twelve years we don't all want to kill each other. Or that we haven't.

I'm working now, I realise, talking to the Captain over mock-chicken and white wine.

"I want you to take the crew over to Erasmus, so that they can see what it's like for themselves."

"Haven't they seen the briefing?"

"Not the same as being there. And if we'd known about your virtual construct, we'd have used it before. Why did you keep it to yourself?"

"It was for Hannah. So she had somewhere she could be real."

"You do see the irony of that, don't you? That she can only be real in a virtual world?"

"She can feel there, and touch."

I notice that polished cutlery and fine food is improving the Captain's table manners. I notice, too, that she has dressed for the occasion in a crisp dress tunic with scarlet braids. Her normally unkempt hair is pressed in place. I wonder why I've only just noticed.

"Yeah, well. I think you're mean for not sharing that technology with the team who developed this mission. It would have helped us with planning, for one thing. Not to mention ship morale. Still, not too late."

"Maybe I don't want to share."

"Ah," she says, laughing, and this time I get the impression she's laughing with me. "But you don't get a choice anymore. Because I'm the Captain, and I know what you've got hidden in that tiny bracelet of yours." I pull down my sleeve to cover the crimson band, but she grabs my hand and looks closely. "Astounding that you can get so much computing power into that little wristband. You'd have thought it would be bigger."

I pull my arm away. "I had to get it past Security. Hannah's not supposed to be here."

Hendricks – Caz – laughs again, a deep throaty laugh which rocks her back in her seat and causes her to reach for her napkin to dab her eyes. "You mean she's a stowaway? And you're a thief?"

"Surely you knew she wasn't supposed to be on the ship?"

"You're paying. I figured you could bring whoever you liked. Besides, she doesn't weigh anything, she doesn't eat anything, and she lives most of the time in that virtual world of hers."

"The Government would never allow me to take her off-planet. She's an asset."

"A miracle of virtual science."

"They want to study her."

"You could have made a copy."

"Then I would have to leave part of her behind." A part of her that would be backed by the full computing power of the planet. A part of her which could fully realise her potential. No, if I left her behind, then the Hannah on the ship would be the copy, and I'd always wonder what I'd sacrificed.

Hannah stays away for two days. She materialises just as I leave the shower, naked and dripping water on the floor. Our showers are communal, and I'm grateful that we are alone.

"You should be careful with that," she says, looking at the puddles. "Strains the recycling systems if you don't drip where you're supposed to." She looks up into my face, and she seems to be ignoring my nakedness. I grab my clothes and, still damp, pull on my trousers.

"Where have you been?" I ask her when we are back in our cabin.

"Working."

"So it's true, then?"

She has her back to me, and looks out of the porthole. "You set the virtual world up so I'd have somewhere to go. Well the world isn't just the stream and the lake and you and me making love under the three moons. It's about all the mundane things that make for a life. Eating, sleeping, peeing, putting out the trash. I have to do all those things, you know. Of course you know – you created this vehicle for me to do all those things. And if you hadn't, I couldn't be human, could I? Because they're all part of the stunningly tedious human existence. So of course I need a job, because in the very real world you created you don't get apartments without money, and you don't get money without working for it. Unless you magically just give me loads of money to start with, which you didn't because that wouldn't have been real, would it? And that would have screwed with all your predictions and projections."

"I thought you spent most of your time in other places."

"Other virtual worlds, you mean? Sure, I spent some time there, once I found out how to slide through the system boundaries. You should have prevented that, you know. Because it gave me experiences the other Hannah could never have."

"And now?"

She turns from the window and looks at my wrist. "Now you've trapped me in that damn bracelet of yours there are only two places I can be. Here with you, or home in V-Erasmus."

"You never called it home before."

"That's because I thought you were the only real thing in my life. And now I realise that the only real thing is myself."

I start to say something, but she is already fading. I like to think there is a tear in her eye, but I suspect it's just a reflection from the porthole.

A week later she hasn't returned. I am furious. It is the Captain's fault. I track her down on the Bridge. She is standing over a console talking to one of the pilots who sits, staring intently at a screen.

"What did you say to her?"

She stops talking to the pilot and looks up. The other members of the Bridge crew – three of them, all men – stop and stare at me. One of them, one of the security detail, reaches for something at his side. I hesitate, but this has gone too far.

She comes over and rests her hand on my shoulder. "Come with me," she whispers, and nods to the pilot. I see the crew relax, though they still glance at me warily. Then the Captain leads me outside and closes the door. We stand out in the corridor.

"She doesn't want to talk to you."

"You've seen her?"

"I don't know what to say."

"You've slept with her, haven't you?" She laughs, though there is no humour. I start to walk away, then turn and walk back. "Have I lost her?"

She sighs. "That, Jim, is up to you." We stand in silence for a few seconds, then she opens the Bridge door and leaves me alone in the corridor. I realise that this is the first time she's called me by my first name, but I'm not ready to begin wondering what that means.

I track her down in the café, the one where the man was smoking the cigar. She is there with a couple of system avatars, male, young, suited. They are laughing at something she says. She looks up, surprised, but recovers her composure quickly. "Jim! Good to see you." She gestures at the spare seat. "Join us." I sit. She introduces me to the avatars. I ignore them. "They're my friends," she will tell me later. I will remind her that they aren't real, but she won't listen. I'm predicting this, of course, because I used to make my living at understanding how things were going to work out so that's what I do. And, suddenly, I know how this situation is going to unfold too.

"You'll excuse me," I say to her, and dematerialise.

She joins me in the cabin five minutes later. "What was that about?"

"You realise it's been two months."

"I wasn't expecting you to take this long to track me down."

"You wanted me to find you?"

"I thought you might have made an effort." She moves towards me, moves her hand towards my shoulder, moves the other to my face. They hover, millimetres from my skin. I feel my hairs tingle.

"I love you," I say.

"Yes." And then she dematerialises.

46

She waits for me beside the lake. I place my hand inside hers and we kiss. It's more metallic than I remember, and the taste is off. But it's her, and I'm hungry for her, and as I lean forward she unbuttons my tunic. She turns me over and presses me down onto the soft grass. Her hair is loose and falls over her face. As she bends over it brushes my cheek, softly caressing me. It should tickle, but it doesn't. Instead it feels like it is seeping down into my flesh, becoming me.

And so it begins again.

In this way we establish the pattern that sees us through the next twelve years. We fall out, make up and fall out all over again. And each time there is more distance between us, more realisation that we are in separate worlds. But I have the power of life or death over her. I can destroy the array, and she will have nowhere to live. I sometimes wonder if that is all that keeps her coming back.

We are two months away from Erasmus now. Tai Ceti lies directly ahead, the brightest star in the sky. We are playing chess in the restaurant. Over the years the crew and passengers have become used to Hannah. Eventually, Caz persuaded me to let them all visit V-Erasmus, and Hannah was a more than willing host. Now when she visits the ship, she visits us all, and I have learned I can't be possessive. Still, she comes to me at night, when it matters the most.

She has my queen and rook in a knight fork. She looks up. "I'll miss this."

I don't know what she's talking about.

"We're close now. It's almost time." And I watch, helpless, as she fades away.

I run from the restaurant and head for my cabin. I grab the headset. It should calibrate on her location, but I know from experience that she can subvert the connection. I emerge in her apartment. It is cold and empty and I realise she hasn't been there for some time. She's not at her office, either, or any of the places we've been to together. I sit on the banks of the lake and cry.

I interact with the programme, talking to the avatars. I shout at her boss, but he doesn't know where she is either. Her colleagues are dismissive. I search all day, then as the light deepens I head down an unfamiliar alleyway, hoping to find her in the bar whose light I can see spilling out into the street. Two men emerge and even in the gloom I recognise them as the two avatars I saw her with in the café, years before. They move towards me until we are standing inches apart. I am about to speak to them when I feel a sharp blow to my stomach. The taller of the two has punched me. I drop to the ground, and the other one kicks me, hard. I wince at the pain. "You bastard," I hear one of them say, as my back spasms from another blow. I should dematerialise, but something stops me. I welcome the next blow. And the next. Before I black out I wonder if I can die there, in Hannah's virtual prison.

I disappoint myself by waking, groggy but unhurt, in my cabin. At first my body is seeped with agonising aches and sharp intense muscular stabs, but it soon wears off as the nerve endings work out that here, back in the real world there is no need for pain. Nevertheless I have a headache so strong that I can hardly think. I limp to the medical room and search the medicine cabinet.

"You were crying out," says Caz from behind me. "Half the ship must have heard you."

"Sorry," I say, as I pop a couple of tablets in my mouth. I swallow them dry. She looks at me, expectantly, so I tell her what happened. She tells me she thinks I let them punish me because I think I deserve it. "Do you think I deserve it?"

She avoids the question, instead picks me up on why I always refer to the inhabitants of V-Erasmus as avatars and not people. "I thought they had to be real, like people, or the simulation wouldn't be real and Hannah wouldn't interact with her world properly. You told me your company was good at that sort of thing."

I realise I've been fooling myself. I already know, of course, but that's how I deal with things. Moments of lucidity followed by denial. "So I've really lost her this time haven't I? To them."

"Probably. But don't take it personally. It's not you."

"I'm her jailer."

"Well, in a way. But she doesn't blame you for that. She hasn't forgotten you made it possible to exist in the first place, even though she started off resenting you for bringing her on this stupid journey."

"What, then?"

"We're nearly there. Erasmus. Where you'll meet the other one." Hannah. The flesh and blood Hannah. "She knows she's going to lose you, Jim. So she's doing what's best for her."

In the remaining days it takes us to reach planetfall I spend almost all my time in V-Erasmus, even though she's not there. I sleep in her apartment, smelling her sheets as I wake. I am always alone, and the bedroom is always cold without her presence.

I sit on the banks of the river. And just as the sun starts to set…

…I wake, abruptly, back in my cabin. The captain looks down at me, holding my wristband. "You need to get up." We're there.

"I didn't know you could do that." I say, pointing at the wristband. "I hope you haven't broken it."

"Don't care if I have. Time for you to get back to the real world." She pockets the wristband and turns her back. I consider objecting, but know it won't get me anywhere. Besides, just as she disappears down the corridor, she calls back. "You can have it back later. If you decide real life's all a bit much to take."

We are in orbit. Every member of the crew seems to be running somewhere, doing something important. Without a role, I slink into the restaurant and sit with a cup of coffee.

Hannah sits opposite me. "Hi." She looks sad. She fiddles with her hair and looks away.

"Why did you leave?"

She glances over at the clock on the wall. "Nearly time. Forgive me this last visit. I guess I'm not as strong as I thought I was." She's crying. And before I can reply she fades.

I wonder if it's the last time I will see her. She's not real, I tell myself, finally, anticipating the Hannah to come.

They put me on the first shuttle to the surface. Erasmus knows we're coming, of course. We've been in contact for almost a month, since we first reached the outer edge of the Virginis system and radio communications became practical. I had missed the steady passing of information between ship and planet, but as we gather ourselves for the descent my professional curiosity begins to return. I review the recordings.

Erasmus is peaceful, just as we'd speculated. And we were right about the war, too. But as I study the images from the surface I realise that whist we may have got the broad thrust of our predictions right, in all the little ways that make a city come alive Jefferson is nothing like we'd imagined.

The humidity hits us first, hot and unpleasant. I'd expected that, but it's still a shock. And then the colours, sharpened in the red spectrum by the sun, larger than it should be. The ground is covered in thick grass and short shrubs, all a faded green close in places to inky black, interspersed with strange yellow shoots. I step down from the shuttle's ramp, and sink a couple of inches into the earth, moisture creeping up to my ankle.

There is a welcoming party, hovering a foot or so off the swampy ground in individual transport vehicles that seem to be little more than seats, footrests and high, white backs. Twenty seven of us have come down in the shuttle, and I slink to the back, anxious to avoid contact.

They treat us well, and at first we are given the illusion of equality. But one prediction I kept from the rest of the ship was that because Erasmus has had many more years of elapsed time than the ship has, there is every chance that in all ways they would be more advanced than we are. A 98% chance in fact.

It gradually becomes obvious to everyone we are museum pieces. We are debriefed politely, by Erasmus' scientists and politicians, invited to lunches and parties and, eventually, allowed to wander at will throughout the vast and sprawling city Jefferson has become. We are even given allowances.

I smile as I sip my cappuccino in a café in a square very much like the one in V-Erasmus I sat in many years ago with Hannah.

"What's so funny?" says Caz, sitting opposite.

"They still use money," I say.

"And why's that so amusing?"

"Because they're not supposed to. Money is supposed to be a way less advanced cultures distribute resources without having to kill each other. Erasmus is supposed to be beyond all that. Means there's hope for us."

Caz gives me an exasperated 'you'd better explain yourself' look.

"It means we're not entirely obsolete. They have a trading culture, so we can trade. Build things. Open restaurants. Give people guided tours of the ship."

"Why? They've given us an allowance. A very generous one."

I finish my drink. "It's not about the money."

But I have no time to build a business empire, at least not yet. And for me it's not really about that, either. I think I'm smiling because I finally realise that there is a limit to my ability to predict the future, and that means that my destiny is not foregone. I begin to hope again.

And that's when I begin my search for Hannah, the Hannah of this world. I had imagined that she would have played a significant role in the development of the colony, and at first I am disappointed that she seemed to fade into anonymity as soon as her father's Mayorship ended. Still, with an active global-net nobody can be completely anonymous and it isn't hard to trace her life. Higher education, then marriage. That stings, but I had prepared myself for that. She would have been too attractive, too vibrant not to attract attention and she had no reason to know that I was coming for her. Divorced seven years later. A daughter, Jade.

She worked right here in Jefferson City, attached to the University. I smile when I read that she became a predictologist. Then, nothing. She drops off the net, during the war. One day there, the next, not.

The Hannah I had anticipated would not have been caught out by anything as trivial as a war. She would have escaped. That's what I had predicted.

But all I can find is a contact number.

A current one.

I dial, if you can call mentally nudging my brand new neural implant 'dialling'.

"Hello," she says, on the third ring, with a voice I'd know anywhere.

"Hannah?"

She laughs, "No, Mr Asher, I'm Jade."

The daughter. Of course. "Then why are you answering her calls?"

Her sigh is loud. "She's not here, Mr Asher."

"When can I speak to her?"

"We should talk."

We sit, hours later, at the top of a tower high over the city. Our bench seats are suspended two feet in the air with no visible support. We have a view of the whole city, covering all the land below, spread so far that the jungle beyond has disappeared over the horizon. If I hadn't seen the pictures from space I might imagine that the whole planet is covered in streets and buildings.

It is not unattractive. The city is carefully landscaped, with lakes and rivers dotted strategically around. And it is mainly transport free too, with the city's main transit systems buried deep underground. The towers gleam in the sunlight.

I spread my hands on the legless table, unsure how to start. The woman sitting opposite me could be Hannah, at least at a distance. Same height, same build, same smile. But the dimples are missing, and her face is pulled back, somehow. But her hair is styled in one of Hannah's - my Hannah's – favourite styles, long extended curls just off the shoulder, and she has the same way of watching me from the corner of her eye even when she's looking at something else.

It is all small talk at first. I ask her how she knows who I am. She shows me how to read the information available through my implant. "You're famous, Mr Asher," she says, "everyone knows who you are."

We are on our second coffee before I begin to talk. We had been regularly beaming updates from Earth on our progress with the Hannah-simulations, so Jade knew I was on the *Celestial Paragon*, and why. That meant Hannah did too.

"How did she react?"

Jade shrugs. "Flattered. Scared. A little intimidated."

I change the subject, desperate to know more but unable to ask. "Tell me about the war."

She leans back. I worry that she will fall off her seat but a seat back rises from somewhere and supports her. "What's to tell? You've read the accounts, seen the vid-reels. We won, they lost, lots of people died."

"Hannah?"

A smile. "That was around the time we found out about the Erasmus flight and the simulation you made of my mother. She worked out she'd be seventy-four by the time you got here." She pauses. "You're a predictologist. You can figure out the rest."

It is three in the morning before it comes to me. I wait for a while and ring her as early as I dare, after fleshing out the details. "She's in space, isn't she?"

"Clever boy. Do you know it's only five-thirty, by the way?"

"When does she get back?"

"In about a year's time. That way she'll be your age when you see her, give or take a decade or so."

"She did that for me?"

Laughter. "They told me all about your narcissism. Don't forget there was a war. It was dangerous here, and she was a scientist. When the space programme offered her an escape, she took it."

"So, it's a coincidence that she's taken an interstellar trip which will slow her ageing down, just like mine did?"

"Entirely. But doesn't the romantic in you want to believe it isn't?."

I might, but something bothers me.

"You were young. She left you behind."

There is no laugh this time. "I was seventeen. I was glad she was gone."

I wonder why, and I begin to feel apprehension.

I spend the year learning. I discover all that I can about my new home and am comforted that reality is subtly different to most of my predictions. At first I am frustrated that Erasmus's technical sophistication places me at a disadvantage, but my minor celebrity status with the academic community means I have access to the latest science, and I begin to take part in professional discussions.

But I'm not involved in the decision to provide a body for V-Hannah. That was, I later discover, Captain

Hendricks. It is a flesh and blood body, too, using a new technique that provides no consciousness until one is downloaded from the virtual world, thus removing any ethical dilemmas.

I am there when she wakes up. She looks right at me, starts to smile, then turns away. Then she asks that I leave the room. She leaves the city almost immediately. She refuses an implant too, deliberately staying disconnected from the global net. I have no idea where she is.

It is for the best, I tell myself. V-Hannah isn't real, despite her new body. Real Hannah is about to return. There would be no place for the simulation.

The research ships return, right on schedule, which seems to surprise everyone except me. The trip had been a great success. They found two new inhabitable planets, and left skeleton colonies behind. Already, new colony ships are being prepared.

I see Hannah as she descends the steps of her shuttle, pushing her greying hair back on her head. I call her name and wave but the crowd is large and I cannot make myself heard.

I don't get to speak to her until the reception. She stands a couple of inches shorter than I'd predicted, a couple of kilos heavier, a glass of champagne in her hand.

"Hello." I say, unsure what to say next.

"You came for me," she says.

"Yes," I reply, looking for her dimples and frowning when they refuse to appear.

"Well that's very flattering," she says in a way which comes across as slightly patronising. "Twelve light years, just for me. And am I what you were expecting?"

"No," I reply, truthfully.

She laughs. "Good. I like to be unpredictable."

We talk about her trip, and she asks me about mine. She seems bored when I try to tell her about Earth. We promise to meet up for coffee in a week or so.

#

She is busy. Then she is ill, suffering the lingering effects of her long space flight. But one day she has no more excuses and agrees to meet me.

When she fails to show at the coffee house I take a transit pod to Jade's apartment, because that's the only place I know that she might be.

There is an uneasy standoff in Jade's living room. The three of us share a bottle of wine and Jade tries unsuccessfully to keep the conversation light.

"That's a nice dress, mama. Suits you."

"It's out of fashion and you know it. I just can't be bothered to buy anything new."

I want to tell Hannah I love her but instead I ask her if she's pleased to be home. She winces for a second or two as though she's got indigestion. I must look alarmed because she stares straight at me and frowns. "What?"

"I thought I knew all your expressions."

"I think, Mr Asher, you're thinking of someone entirely different."

I start to protest. Hannah gives me a piercing stare and raises her arm.

"Oh stop. You are so socially inept no woman will go out with you. So you develop a fixation with a copy of me and fool yourself you're in love with it, just because you've not programmed her to say no. Then you go on a stupid romantic quest for the real thing – me – thinking I'll love you just as much as you got your virtual plaything to do. Am I right?"

I say nothing, though I suspect my cheeks are reddening. I look around to Jade for support. She is looking at her shoes.

"Then when you get here you dump the simulation, even though you said you were in love with her."

That much is true, I realise.

"And you wonder why you creep me out?"

I look across at the stranger who looks a little like Hannah and know that I don't love this woman at all. I wonder why I ever thought I did.

This pale copy of my Hannah is right, I conclude. I have allowed my fixations, my insecurities and my arrogance to cloud my judgement for the whole of my life.

Caz laughs when I tell her. She is running charter flights to the planet's polar ski resorts, using one of the *Celestial Paragon's* shuttles. A comedown from piloting a starship, but at least she gets to do some skiing. "Took you long enough to work that out, superbrain."

"That's not even accurate, anymore. Everyone else's Next-Gen enhancements mean I'm virtually a moron here."

"Me too," she says. "Doesn't mean you have to be unhappy though. Maybe now you won't feel the urge to overthink everything, and you can just get on with what makes you feel good. Fancy a ski trip?" I'm about to say yes when she adds. "Someone there you might like to get reacquainted with."

She is real now, I know that. "She ran away from me."

"That's true. You didn't make her feel good." I reflect on that. I argue that's because I had a fundamental misunderstanding of what constitutes reality. Caz counters that was because I was an arse. I believe both statements to be true.

"Do you think she ever wanted to be with me? Or was it just that she had no choice?"

"Why don't you find out?"

The shuttle departs the next morning, packed with Jefferson's holidaying elite, And me. I hardly notice the journey, don't even look out of the window when Caz points out all the supposedly fantastic landmarks on our route. My mind is full of Hannah.

When the shuttle touches down I am first by the doors, eager to find her. Caz stops me by deliberately hanging on to my bags. I think about leaving them, but the temperature is below freezing and I need my warm weather clothes.

"What's your hurry?" says Caz, dangling my bag.

I need to locate Hannah. Nothing else matters. "I need to…"

"Relax," she interrupts. "She's not going anywhere."

"You know where she is."

"And when you're ready, I'll tell you."

I argue, but she persuades me that I have to pace myself. I think she just wants someone to go skiing with. I contemplate hating her, but she's grinning at me and I find it difficult to be angry, I settle for exasperation, but I realise I have no choice. There are three hundred square miles of skiing and Hannah could be anywhere. I need Caz's help.

She's better at skiing than me, but she doesn't seem to mind. The skiing is good. I thought first that I'd have forgotten how, but two or three mild falls in, I felt ready to try the most difficult slopes and, surprising myself, I begin skiing with confidence and, I like to fool myself, style. For the first time since arriving on Erasmus I feel exhilarated. Something else, too. I am content.

I find Hannah behind a bar in a mountainside chalet. She pours me a beer. "Took you long enough."

She has her hair in long ringlets, falling onto her shoulders. "Hannah," I say, embracing the thrill of saying her name out loud but apprehensive about her reaction.

"Jim," she replies. "Here for me?" I nod. She looks away. "I don't need you anymore."

"I was hoping…"

"Hoping that I really like you and I wasn't just with you because you gave me no choice?"

"But…"

"Hoping I would want you now I'm a real person?"

"But…"

"Hoping that I wouldn't care that now you've been rejected by the original Hannah you want to come back to the imitation?"

All this is true, I realise. I leave my beer and head for the door.

"Wait."

I turn, expectant.

"You haven't paid for your drink."

Caz waits outside, stamping her feet to keep warm. She holds my skis out to me.

"Went well, eh?"

"You shouldn't have waited, I could have been a while," I say, but I can sense that she knows better.

We ski, silently, for hours, until it begins to get dark. At dinner, later, we dissect the day. The food is bland and the drink tasteless.

"You had to find out, you know," she says.

"Why?"

"Because when you're not being a delusional dick you have potential." Normally I find her insult/compliments amusing. This one I just find perplexing. But she has lifted the tension and I begin to relax.

The shuttle is due to leave the next morning. "You going to be on it?" she asks.

I don't reply. Hannah doesn't want me so I should leave. But I love Hannah so I should stay and fight for her.

"Not ready to let her go yet, then?"

Hannah knocks on my door just as I am getting ready for bed.

"Hello," she says. I let her in.

My room is sparsely furnished, Alpine style, all light wood and coarse fabrics. There is enough room for a chair and a bed. I sit on the chair, Hannah takes the bed. We sit, quietly, for a long time, then Hannah coughs and breaks the spell.

"Despite myself, I still want you," she says. "I know it's not your fault I was dependent on you. But I had no choice."

"I had no choice either. Not if I was to give you life."

"And I'm grateful for that. But I shouldn't have come here. Because I need to move on."

"Why did you?"

"Because I still need you."

And that's when I get it. "No, you really don't," I say. We talk some more, cry a little then come to a mutual understanding, and then I walk her to the door. I hug her as she leaves and I watch her as she walks slowly down the corridor, not looking back. I used to think of her as my Hannah, but she never was. And now I've set her free.

I don't get much of a chance to speak to Caz on the way back to the city, because she's busy flying the shuttle and I'm busy trying to persuade myself I haven't made a big mistake. Actually what I feel most is relief, because I know I'm finally free of the self-imposed obsessional prison I'd put myself in. She's there when we land though, on the tarmac, holding my bag.

"Got anyplace I should be taking this?" I hold out my hand to take the bag. She snatches it away and grins. "I'll just keep it at my place, then." She strolls away.

"Why?"

Caz turns back. "Because then I'll have control over you. You'll have to come and see me to get your things back." There is something pleasing about the way she walks that I hadn't noticed before.

"I could just leave them with you. I don't need ski clothes in the city."

"But you won't. Because I have what you really want."

It takes me a moment to get her meaning, then I realise she's waiting for me to follow. And now I can see it. No longer obsessed with Hannah, I notice what should have been obvious all along. I linger over the thought, and find I like it.

"You flirting with me? Only I'm confused, because aren't you supposed to be gay?"

She laughs. "You really don't understand women, do you?"

She's right.

I don't.

Certainty

Venn Rand tried not to listen, but it was hard with everyone yelling at him.

"We're not paying you to take detours," the Acolyte said.

"Screw that, there's salvage down there," said Zoe.

"There are life signs," said Sevvie, the androgynous ship's AI.

The Priestess just smiled.

Zoe and Sevvie were crew, the Priestess and her acolyte paying guests. That didn't mean Venn had to like them, or be polite. "Shut up and let me think," he said.

Venn's ship, the *Diamante*, was low on fuel and half way to where they needed to be, so they were in orbit round a glorified asteroid that surveyed positive for supplies. They weren't expecting any other ships, and yet, there it was.

They all stood in a circle and stared at the image the external sensors projected in the air between them. A ship, slightly lower orbit, same trajectory. They could be in and out in a couple of hours. Ugly, squat and gunmetal. Military, obviously. But what was it doing, so far from home?

"You said this area of space was uninhabited." The Acolyte paced, difficult in a cramped cabin with a low ceiling, particularly in a long heavy woollen robe with the hood up. He had to stoop to avoid the pipework.

"I said the place wasn't fully settled. You should listen more." Not for the first time in the three weeks since they'd set out, Venn wondered whether anyone would care if he just shoved the Acolyte out of the airlock. He suspected even the Priestess would carry on smiling. "There's a small mining colony. How else do you think they extract the minerals we need to run this thing? You think there are power cells lying around on the ground like big boulders waiting for us to pick them up?"

"That doesn't look like a mining ship." The Acolyte tried to cross his arms but snagged his robes on the plate Venn had eaten his stale pizza off. It crashed, joining the rest of the debris on the cabin floor. He stared down for a moment and curled his bottom lip.

"There's a hole at the back where one of the engines used to be." Venn waved his arm and the image grew larger.

"Meteor?" Zoe said. She was short and wiry, with close cropped black hair and an intense expression on her face.

"Even more reason to be on our way," said the Acolyte. "There may be danger."

"What exactly is the tearing hurry?" Venn didn't really want an answer. The religious people didn't talk much, and mostly that was fine, because it meant he didn't have to listen to them. They paid enough to do anything they wanted to, more or less, and that included not answering questions.

The only thing he'd insisted on was taking Sevvie with them. They protested and spouted some nonsense about how AIs represented man's hubris for trying to play god and we were all going to hell. Only their god could create smarts, it seems, and then only in his own image. The complete lack of aliens in the universe only reinforced that belief. But without Sevvie there was no way Venn could get the ship to work, so eventually they relented, not that they were happy about it.

Zoe brought up some schematics, and stacked them on the image. "There's still life support, though most of the atmosphere seems to have vented. But the life signs are in the cargo deck, where there wasn't any air in the first place."

"They must be suited," the Acolyte said.

"Which means that whatever happened was recent," said Zoe.

Venn turned to Sevvie. "How long?"

"Suits on a military transit have more air reserves than conventional ones. It is fair to assume that they will be well maintained with full tanks."

"The quick version?"

"Twelve hours, give or take an hour or so depending on how much energy they use. If they stay still and don't talk, maybe fourteen."

"Anyone else out here?"

Sevvie shook his head. "We're all they've got."

The Acolyte looked up. "You're going to listen to a Mark Seven robot?"

Venn didn't know why Sevvie put up with the insults. Not worth it, probably. He and Zoe nodded at each other, and Sevvie manipulated the numbers on the display. They were going in.

Venn wasn't going to risk moving the *Diamante* too close to the military ship so they took a shuttle and docked carefully, entering though the airlock. The Acolyte insisted on coming, but that didn't mean Venn and Zoe had to wait for him. They were used to zero-g and the religious man evidently wasn't. Curses through the comms relay made Venn laugh. Not very saintly.

Once they turned the corner to head for the control room they floated into darkness. Venn and Zoe switched on their head lamps. After a while, no doubt after he'd worked out how to do it, the Acolyte's torch switched on too.

The fact that the gravity was off was a worry. A ship like this had emergency redundancies, but for some reason they hadn't kicked in. And with the lights off, the whole place had a cold stillness about it. The corridor was cramped and low, which didn't help, more a tube really with a flat bottom where the floor used to be, pipes and handholds everywhere. Grey. No frills. That meant this was a battle ship, built for fighting. There was air at first, but one closed bulkhead later, and they were in hard vacuum.

"What's this ship doing here?" said Zoe.

"Refuelling, maybe. Just like us."

"You think?"

"No."

The door to the control room was open. Venn didn't know much about military ships, but he knew enough to know that was wrong.

"This has been blasted." Zoe glided over and poked at the warped metal. The door was maybe six inches of something very solid, designed to keep the control room secure even if the ship were boarded. And yet there it was, open.

"Careful."

"Don't worry," said Zoe. "You're going in first."

The Acolyte caught up. "We need to leave."

That was probably the only half-sensible thing Venn could remember the Acolyte saying. Now he'd had time to think about it he knew he'd been foolish to think they could get salvage from a military ship without someone wondering where he'd got it from. But there were those life signs to think about. And the need to disagree with a anything the Acolyte said. On principle.

He could hear Zoe, just behind him. "You leave then."

"This ship has been attacked! Whoever did this could still be here!" said the panicked Acolyte.

Venn took in the surroundings. Bigger than the control room of the *Diamante*, which left room for more people. And there they were, slumped over chairs, floating up to the ceiling, impaled on bits of machinery. Venn counted five bodies, none suited, all with blast injuries. The central console was a pile of seared plastic.

"Sevvie," Venn activated his ship-to-ship. "You still registering life signs?"

"Still there. Three of them. One deck down from you, a hundred metres towards the rear."

"I need to know more about what this ship was up to. Roster, mission, that sort of thing."

"It's not on the database, which is unusual. Even the clandestine ships are usually listed, if you know where to look. Not this one. It's a modified Class Five, which means it probably had a crew compliment of around one hundred, and some heavy weaponry."

"Modified?"

"The cargo bay, where the life signs are, doesn't match the Class Five design. There's some non-standard equipment there. That affects the weight, so there are some structural compensations."

"Ideas?"

"Somebody's put a tank in there, and installed fancy tech around it. I'm registering some interesting gases in there too inside the tank itself. Mainly nitrogen but with concentrations of hydrogen and methane. Neon too, and argon. No oxygen, No hydrocarbons."

"An atmosphere tank, then. For what?" Venn glanced across at the Acolyte. "Is it full?"

"There's certainly something in there, aside from the atmosphere," said Sevvie.

The Acolyte pulled him by the arm. "We have to get out of here," the religious man said, talking rapidly.

Now that the bodies had started to pile up, Venn's curiosity was completely satisfied, but he couldn't just ignore those life signs. He sighed and checked his pulse pistol. Nice toy, but they'd need more. Zoe was ahead of him. She projected her viewscreen and pulled up a ship plan. She traced her finger to a point just down the corridor. "Weapons are here."

"Can you fix the lights?"

"If we had time I could run a power patch from the shuttle," said Zoe.

"I can do that remotely," said Sevvie.

"Do it."

"On it. Be careful."

The weapons room was open. Some large gaps showed where heavy duty stuff had been hastily removed. Not all of it, though. Venn picked a large pulse rifle. Zoe went for something smaller and more manoeuvrable. The Acolyte filled his pockets with something, grenades, probably, and went for a repeating missile launcher. Venn gently pushed it aside. "You could blow this whole ship apart with one of those. Try something smaller."

The Acolyte snatched his weapon away. Venn decided not to force the issue. They found more bodies in the corridor leading to the cargo bay. This tunnel was wider, maybe four metres across and as many high, another thing not on the standard schematics. The body count grew the closer they got to the entrance.

"Firefight," said Venn.

"I only see the guys from the ship here," Zoe said.

"Guess they lost, then."

The cargo door was still closed, but there was a hole carved right in it. Not quite man sized, but not small either. Venn figured that Zoe could probably make it through if she didn't have her enviro-suit on. He pushed some bodies aside and peered through. There were bodies in there too, though he couldn't see well enough to count them. The cargo bay was large, big enough to hold the *Diamante* if it needed to. In the middle was a tank the size of a truck, filled with something murky. His shoulder twitched, like it always did when he knew he should be somewhere else.

Then the lights came on.

"Good work, Sevvie. Can you get us gravity?"

"There's not enough power for that. But I can get that door open for you. Just give me a while."

The Acolyte's facemask was a gold covered mirror, but close up Venn could just about see inside. A worried face looked back. Venn knew he shouldn't, but he couldn't resist. "What do you think we'll find in there?"

"Venn!" Zoe said through their private channel. He didn't need to see her to know she was scowling.

"Quiet. Having fun."

"Obviously these men fell out with each other for some reason. Maybe fell out over their mission." The Acolyte turned away.

"What do you think is in the tank, then?" said Venn,

"Nothing. They must be using it to test atmosphere suits." The Acolyte sounded irritated.

"You think?"

"What other explanation could there be?"

"You certain?" Venn was goading him now.

"If you believed, you'd be certain too."

Just then, the door opened. If there had been any atmosphere in the corridor, Venn was sure he would have heard the metal wrench and tear past the blast damage.

Inside, more bodies floated high to the ceiling. Some were in enviro-suits, some in their combat clothing Most times military men were a mix of the fit and the fat, guys in shape and guys struggling to keep up. Not these men. They all looked super-athletic, with military buzz cuts and the kind of musculature that takes serious work. A crack team, then. There was grim determination there, behind their empty eyes. Something else too. Maybe that's what terror looked like.

"You still registering life signs?" Venn tapped his helmet when all he got back was static. "Something's interfering with the ship-to-ship," he said to Zoe.

"Connected with the tank, probably. Remember we couldn't get full detail on the life signs before?"

"Maybe." Venn hoped that was all it was. They moved closer to the gas-filled chamber, still opaque even in the full glare of the bay spotlights. The Acolyte hung back.

Zoe was up against the glass now, looking in. Venn joined her. There were shapes in there, through the gloom. Bodies. Five, maybe six. Without knowing how many limbs they were supposed to have it was hard to tell, because they were floating, tangled up like dead lovers. But one thing was clear. They weren't human. "So, we're not alone after all."

"I'm not listening to this," said the Acolyte, from the doorway.

Venn turned to Zoe. "What do you think happened here?"

She took a few seconds to answer. "They're wearing clothing. That means they're probably intelligent."

"What killed them?"

"Who knows. The firefight maybe. Or when the power went off, perhaps their atmosphere degraded." Zoe shrugged. Even in her environment suit, Venn could see that. "First contact."

"They have to be alive for that."

"But we know they're there now, right?" said Zoe.

"Tell that to him." Venn gestured over to the Acolyte, pacing around by the door.

"See nothing, worry about nothing." Zoe edged up the glass and peered down through the roof.

"We should leave."

Zoe nodded. "I've got all this recorded. We can try and make sense of it later."

They turned to go. By the time they reached the doorway, the Acolyte was halfway down the corridor.

Venn turned. "Hear that?"

Zoe looked at him, faceplate to faceplate. "No atmosphere, no sound. Remember?"

"Feel it then."

"Don't get weird on me."

He remembered the life signs and how vague they were. He turned and headed back towards the tank.

"That's a really stupid idea," Zoe said.

He looked back, saw her hesitate then follow. The Acolyte was already out of sight.

Something on the edge of his vision, to the right. Then to the left. He fingered the safety catch on his weapon. Then stillness. He hoped he was imagining things.

It happened fast. A blur, far away at the back of the bay, then closer. Over him, round him, in front, closing rapidly.

Then Zoe fired her pistol, and it twitched and shifted direction. Still coming, but spinning now. It hit him on the shoulder, hard.

Venn fell, as whatever had hit him smash against the wall, unable to turn in the zero-g. It bounced off. Between Zoe's shot and the impact, Venn didn't think anything could have survived.

"You ok?"

"Yes."

"Good. There may be more. *Three* life signs, remember?"

Venn got to his feet and looked around. Nothing but floating bodies and a great big tank filled with mysteries. One of the bodies, the one which had clattered into Venn, had six limbs and a tail. Zoe dragged it over.

Whatever was inside was dead now. It was small, maybe four feet in length, and wearing some sort of space suit. If he'd been a scientist, Venn would have opened it up and taken a look inside, but there was no time for that, especially if more of them were around. Besides, the helmet suggested the thing's face was long and thin. Like a velociraptor. Some things you don't want to see.

"Definitely intelligent then. This space suit looks more advanced than ours." Venn peered into the creature's facemask.

"We put monkeys in space back in the 20th century. They wore space suits too."

Movement.

"Over there." Zoe indicated to her right.

Venn raised his gun, then lowered it. "One of the military guys." The side wall was draped with ropes. He grabbed one to steady himself. The soldier was above him now, and he looked up into the faceplate. "A woman. Looks like she's unconscious."

"Can't have much air left."

Venn nodded. "We need to wake her."

"Not here." So they dragged her through the corridors back to the shuttle. As soon as they were through the airlock, Zoe unclasped her mask, then leaned over and unfastened the soldier's.

"Where's the Acolyte?" said Venn.

"Maybe one of the aliens got him. There might be another one out there, remember?"

"I don't like the idea of a killer alien running loose. Can't say I'm bothered about the Acolyte, though."

"Nor me. Does that make us bad people?"

"Probably. What about her?" Venn looked down. She was young with short cropped hair in the military style. She had a tribal tattoo across her left cheek and scars on her neck and chin. And she was waking up.

They hurried back in the shuttle. The woman was called Evans, and she was just winded. She guessed she'd been left for dead by the creatures. "You saw what was in that tank. Their buddies came for them."

"But they're still there."

"They'd been dead almost from the start. That wasn't the plan but our scientists screwed up with the tank's atmosphere. Missing some sort of trace element, apparently. Trouble was, we didn't have any. So that was it."

"Where are they from?"

"That would be telling, now wouldn't it? Need to know. And you don't."

Venn wanted to argue but they needed to get out of there. "Then let's go." Zoe was already prepping the shuttle. Venn tried getting hold of the Acolyte on the short-range but didn't get a reply. That meant either he was dead or the comms interference was getting worse. Probably both. Venn felt bad that the guy was missing but not suicidal enough to go after him. So he pulled up the flight information onto a holoimage projected in front of him, and started the initiation sequence. The engines started to whine.

The image froze, pixelated then faded and Venn found himself staring at the far wall. The engine noise dropped to a murmur. "What just happened?"

Zoe turned and frowned. Then someone started to operate the airlock – from the other side. Someone – or something – was coming in from the military ship.

"The Acolyte?" But that didn't explain why the start-up sequence had aborted. Venn reached for his weapon. It wasn't there.

Someone they'd never seen before dressed in combats and with the same tribal tattoos as Evans walked out of the airlock. He unclipped his helmet one handed. In the other hand he held a pistol.

The third life sign was human.

"Nothing personal," the new arrival said, expressionless. Venn was too distracted by him to notice Evans moving fast, until she too stood in front of him, clicking the safety on a gun which should have been firmly strapped to Venn's thigh.

Venn thought about rushing them, figured it was pointless, waited to see what happened.

But Zoe was already on the move, dropping to the ground. Both Evans and the new guy had been targeting Venn. Now they both turned. "Get moving, you idiot," Zoe yelled. "Can't you see they're going to kill us?"

Venn ducked behind his flight seat. Evans kicked Zoe in the side, flipped her over and raised her gun. Venn peered up to see the military man looking down at him, gun pointed, grinning.

Venn closed his eyes and waited for the sound of the trigger.

And that's when the room exploded

First the noise, then the heat, like standing too close to a jet engine. The light, too, an intense flash that forced his eyes shut. It felt like a punch to the head. But he was behind the chair, and whatever had happened was on the other side. The military guy wasn't so fortunate. Something big and hard sliced right through him, sending him flying against the bulkhead. Venn crouched as debris flew over him, embedding itself in chunks wherever it hit. He was lucky. The blast was high, and he was low. And after a while, things stopped moving.

He got up, slowly, rubbing his eyes. His ears rang like he'd been right under a speaker stack. His body ached too. His enviro-suit was abraded, down to the cloth in places. But it was whole.

Movement from where Evans and Zoe had been. A groan.

"What happened?" Zoe.

"You ok?"

"My arm feels like it's broken. Something wrong with my leg, too."

"Evans?" But he didn't need to wait for the answer. Something had impaled her, just below the clavicle. She stared, glassy-eyed. Not moving.

Dust settled, leaving a clear sight of whatever had exploded. Pieces of thick painted metal, and toughened glass. "That's the airlock door."

"And most of the airlock." Zoe eased herself upright and winced.

"Clamps held, though."

"Or we'd be dead."

"What do you suppose happened?" Venn walked over to where the jagged remains of the shuttle's shattered airlock door now led straight into the larger vessel.

"Remember the Acolyte stuffing things in his pocket when we were in the weapons room? Grenades."

"You think he used one?"

"More than one. Those airlock doors are strong. Good job, too. If they hadn't been there to absorb the force of the blast, we'd be dead as well."

"Tried to kill us then. Destroy the evidence." Venn turned his attention to getting back to the *Diamante*. He tried the ship-to-ship and cursed when he got static in return. "We're on our own."

"And we can't undock the ship because that would leave a hole where the airlock was."

"We were lucky." Zoe rubbed her injured arm and grimaced.

"How do you figure that?"

"There was air in the section we docked with."

And then the shuttle's gravity switched off. "Shit."

"Actually that's helpful," said Zoe. "Zero-g Makes it easier to move around when half your limbs are broken. So?"

"What?"

"Plan?" Zoe had that expectant look.

Nothing like imminent death to focus the mind. "Zoe, you still got the schema of this ship on your system?"

"Sure."

"Does it show where the escape pods are?"

She grinned. "Genius."

They changed suits because theirs were pockmarked and torn. The new ones were one size fits all, too loose in some places, too tight in others. Venn didn't want to think what Zoe's must feel like. He just hoped it didn't chafe her injuries. They'd used a pain suppressant on both her arm and her leg but that wasn't nearly enough. The arm was definitely broken.

The pods in the military ship were all there. It was clear that none of the crew had tried to use them. Venn shook his head. The military mind. The pods were on independent power sources, though Venn didn't quite believe they would work until Zoe powered one up. Whatever had drained the ship had not affected the pod.

The pod had limited thruster capability and Venn managed to steer it to the *Daimante*. As they approached, the bulkhead door opened and a force grapple pulled them in.

Two hours later they sat round a large circular table in the dining area, eating hastily assembled quesadillas and drinking beer. Zoe's arm was in a makeshift sling. Sevvie wasn't drinking, even though he could, and neither was the Priestess, even though Venn knew that she did, back in her room.

They worked around the subject, until Venn got bored with small talk. He turned to the Priestess. "You knew, didn't you? About the aliens."

The smile didn't waver. "That would be impossible. The Book is quite clear on that."

Zoe belched and Venn looked away. Good thing he didn't employ her for her table manners. "I saw one. Right in front of me. Six legs and a face like a crocodile. Bad breath too, probably."

"You must have been mistaken. You were low on oxygen, correct?" The Priestess talked quietly but firmly.

Venn sighed. If the Priestess' religion depended on man being made in god's image, and intelligence only being possible through god's will, then smart lizards were always going to lead to some serious cognitive dissonance. Maybe she told the Acolyte to blow the airlock. Maybe he was just using his initiative. Whatever. She wasn't about to confess and he couldn't prove anything.

It didn't matter much anyway. They had video feed of the aliens and a whole container full of dead ones on the Class Five, just waiting to be picked up and dissected.

And that's when the shockwave hit, and hit hard. Three seconds of mayhem, table scattered, Zoe thrown against Venn's chair back, Sevvie flung to the ceiling. Then the alignment protocols kicked in and the ship righted itself.

Zoe was unconscious. Venn felt for a pulse and relaxed slightly. Sevvie pulled a piece of metal from his arm. There was no sign of the Priestess.

"What just happened?" said Venn.

Sevvie frowned and tried to activate the view-screen. "The external sensor arrays have been overloaded."

"Guesses?"

"The Class Five. We have backup sensors embedded in the hull. I'm bringing them up."

There was space where the Class Five had been. Debris, too, but nothing larger than a football. Maybe the Acolyte had found the self destruct. He had been carrying enough heavy weaponry he probably didn't need it. No ship, no evidence, and no threat to the Church.

Except for Venn and Zoe. They'd seen what happened. And the Priestess must know they had video evidence. And in the confusion, she was gone.

No doubt looking for a way to kill them all.

"Sevvie, can you isolate the engines?"

"Ahead of you. It's the logical move." Sevvie winced. "She's shutting me out."

"Can she blow us up?"

"She's already locked the sequence."

Venn kicked down the door to the Priestess' quarters. She sat on her bed, draped in purple, staring at her array's projection.

"This ship will explode in five minutes, unless you stop it. You willing to die for your beliefs?"

"There were lies on that ship. Lies on your cameras, too. I can't let you return to Earth to spread those falsehoods and undermine the Message."

"How do you know I haven't already transmitted the data?"

"Because long range communications are down."

"Convenient. You, I suppose?"

"I had no idea you were going to bring falsehoods from the military ship. I assume it's your robot, malfunctioning."

"He's not a robot."

Sevvie pushed past Venn and bent down in front of the Priestess. He glared at her with something in his expression Venn had never seen before. Anger.

"You think I'm a robot? An unthinking machine?"

"Man created you. You're in *our* image, not god's. And only god can give life."

"But I'm real, I'm here."

"You have no right to exist."

"And yet I do." He grabbed her by the arms and squeezed.

Venn could see her face tighten. "Stop it, Sevvie. You're hurting her."

Sevvie's anger turned to rage. "She deserves to be hurt. She's going to kill us all. I'm not ready to die."

"How can you die? You have to be alive to die," said the Priestess.

Sevvie released her. "She's trying to erase all traces of first contact and she's too blind to see the evidence of it right in front of her eyes."

Venn looked at the display. "We've got less than a minute."

"And if she blows us up, so what? There are thirteen million AI's operating in the known systems."

"Thirteen million machines," said the Priestess.

"Thirteen million people who have just as much right to live as you have."

"The Book is clear."

"The Book can be rewritten, now we know the truth."

"Thirty seconds," said Venn.

"Can you still be so certain?" Sevvie shook now. If he wasn't chalk white, Venn was sure he would be red in the face.

"There can be no 'first contact'."

"There already has been," said Sevvie. "You're looking at it."

She sat, staring at the control screen, as Venn watched the numbers tick down. Then her face fell. Venn braced himself.

She entered a code sequence then waved her arms. The viewscreen faded.

Then she buried her head in her hands and cried.

They sat, drinking coffee. The Priestess looked uncomfortable. Her eyes were red and she didn't look as though she had slept. Her hair, usually tightly controlled, swept forward in an unruly tangle.

Zoe had a large bruise on her forehead and a sling over her left arm. Sevvie looked smug.

"You were never going to keep the existence of those aliens secret for long," Venn said, sipping his coffee. "Military secrets don't stay secret for ever."

"They'll be back, too," said Zoe. "Now that they know what we do to them."

"If you want your Church to survive, you need some new certainties," said Sevvie. "Then I might even join."

The Priestess shifted in her seat. "What will you do to me?"

Venn laughed. "Nothing at all. You paid for passage. When we arrive we say goodbye. That's it. What you do with your new-found understanding is up to you."

"But you'll tell the authorities about the aliens."

Sevvie frowned. "I don't think we'll have to," he said, opening his screen up in front of them. "Remember our long-range communications are down? I know why, now."

Venn followed everyone else and looked up at the screen.

"*They* blocked them."

The rapidly approaching alien ship was huge. And it was coming straight for them.

"Oh shit," said Venn.

"Amen to that," said the Priestess.

Spirit

Jerry woke up in a brightly lit unfamiliar room and felt a surge of relief. At least if he was in hospital he wasn't dead. The last thing he remembered was the truck, coming right at him at the intersection.

He tried sitting up and immediately felt sick. He wasn't ready for rapid movement. He was wearing a garment like a hospital smock, in a washed out grey colour which blended perfectly with its surroundings. He lay on what he assumed was a hospital gurney. But there wasn't any of the usual hospital equipment around, and there weren't any nurses.

He closed his eyes for a second. He must have slept, because there was a trolley straddling the bed with a plate of food on it filled with what appeared to be meat and a pale mush which he assumed was mashed potato. Next to it was a glass of water and a napkin but no cutlery. Still no nurses.

He ate quickly, scooping the mash with the meat. The mashed potato turned out not to be potato at all and he couldn't identify the meat, or even tell if it <u>was</u> meat. It had an odd salty taste and was seasoned with something unusual. He was too hungry to decide whether or not it was pleasant.

"Hello," someone said. He turned to see a woman looking at him. She was dressed in a white uniform consisting of a jacket with a high collar and knee length skirt over white boots which came up to just above her hem line. Blonde hair hung freely on her shoulders, which wasn't how he expected nurses to wear it. She was pale and wearing no makeup.

"Hello," he said. "What happened to me?"

The woman smiled, but said nothing. He considered repeating his question but then she turned abruptly and, walking awkwardly, headed for the door. It opened automatically and she left, leaving him alone. He couldn't see what was beyond.

He slept.

The next time he awoke there was more food. And at the end of the bed the woman stood, smiling. She angled her head slightly to one side. "Hello."

"Hello," he replied. He looked at the food. "Could I have some cutlery, do you think?"

The woman contemplated the question. "Cutlery," she said. Then she turned and left the room. Jerry looked at the meal. It was the same pseudo-meat and pseudo-potato. He waited for her to return, which she did, with a pair of chopsticks.

Jerry looked at them with an expression that mirrored his confusion. Then he picked the meat up and scooped the potato as before adding, between mouthfuls. "Cutlery, you know. Knife and fork." He mimed holding the meat down with his imaginary fork, cutting a piece off with his imaginary knife and lifting the imaginary chunk to his lips. He mimed chewing appreciatively. "Next time, eh?"

The woman looked alarmed and rushed out of the room, leaving him alone. He had nothing to do, so he thought about the World Series and Sarah Palin and the size of his mortgage and the size of the hole in his bank account Dee Dee had left when she cleaned him out. He had his eyes closed and was imagining how satisfying it would be to use a sharp pair of scissors on Dee Dee's expensive dresses when the woman came back into the room.

He heard the door click shut. He leaned up on the bed. The woman looked like she wanted to say something but she hung back. He tried to decide how old she was. It was impossible to tell. Young, he decided, mainly because he wanted her to be. Foreign, too, because she didn't seem to speak English.

"Do you want the things? I've finished with the things." He said, indicating the remains of his meal. She walked over and removed the tray, standing it against the wall next to the door.

"Thank you," he said.

"You're welcome," she replied.

"You speak English?" He was startled.

"Of course."

"Then why the chopsticks?"

"It was a…" she seemed to struggle for the words "…a calibration error." Her smile broke.

Jerry found he enjoyed her unease. "And another thing." He paused for dramatic effect. "I need to go to the bathroom."

"Of course." Her smile switched on and she fixed her eyes on his. After a few seconds he heard the dull whirr of machinery, and a cubicle descended from the ceiling. It was an enclosed circular column with transparent glass door and walls. Inside were a toilet bowl and sink in the same transparent material, both clearly visible.

"Your bathroom."

"How did you do that? Never mind." He started to scrabble from the bed, then paused.

"Erm. I don't want to be rude, but…?"

"Yes?"

"I need to, you know…"

"Is the cubicle not adequate for your needs?"

"It looks just fine. Apart from the complete lack of privacy." She continued to look at him with her beaming smile, but he thought he could see some uncertainty in her eyes. "Do you understand?"

She stood there unmoving for ten seconds, looking vacantly in his direction. Then she spoke. "Of course. So sorry." She turned and headed out of the door.

He bent to peer at the cubicle. It was a design he didn't recognise and it wasn't clear how the flushing mechanism worked. If indeed there was one. There wasn't any toilet paper either.

He sat back on the bed, feeling mean for embarrassing the woman. She made him uneasy. She was going to want to give him answers to the thousand questions he'd been formulating ever since he woke up. He felt safer without answers.

"Hello," she said. He hadn't noticed her come back in. As she walked towards him the bathroom began a slow rise into its storage cavity. When it had finished he couldn't see any lines or marks on the unblemished white ceiling.

"What happens when you're not around to bring it down?"

"Bring it down?"

"Summon it, Call it to materialise."

"Ah. When you want it, it will be there."

"Like magic?"

She laughed. "Like magic." That was the first time he's seen her laugh. He liked it.

"Can I ask you a question?"

She hesitated. "Yes."

"What's your name?"

"I… let me think about that."

"Think about your name?"

"Yes."

He sighed. "Another question, then. Are we in a hospital?"

"Does it please you to think you might be in a hospital?"

"Well if I'd been involved in a car crash that's exactly where I'd want to be."

"Then think of this as a hospital."

"It's not, though, is it?"

"It is many things."

"And I wasn't in a car crash, was I?"

"You were unconscious for some time," she said, not quite answering his question.

He looked at her hands. They were small and practically unlined, with perfect nails. She had a sweet but

84

naggingly indistinct scent that he was having difficulty placing.

"Who are you?"

She looked startled, looked down and brushed something off her immaculate white skirt. "You must be tired."

"Not really," he started to say. But she had already left the room.

The next time she came in she was holding a tray of food. He leaned forward and took it off her, noting the knife and fork positioned either side of the plate. He wasn't surprised to see the knife on the wrong side.

"Cutlery. Thank you."

"You're welcome." She sat down on the edge of the bed. Her gaze moved quickly from his plate, his hands and his face. "My name is Oprah."

Most unlikely, he thought. But entirely in keeping with the general weirdness. "You going to watch me eat?" he said, with his fork halfway to his mouth.

"If you don't mind."

He shrugged. "I don't mind."

He ate in silence. When he felt thirsty the woman handed him the glass of water. When he had finished the woman passed him the napkin and took his tray away.

"Tell me," he said, when she had repositioned herself at the end of his bed. "What is that meat?"

"Meat?"

"You know, solid brown thing. Next to the potatoes."

"Potatoes?"

He sighed. "Okay, let me rephrase the question. What food have I been eating?"

"You don't like it?"

"I didn't say that. Although, to be honest, a bit of variety would help."

"Sorry" her face fell.

"Don't sweat it. I'm just curious, that's all. It's not beef, though it tastes a bit like beef. Just wondering."

"It's not meat."

"Figured. What is it, then?"

"It's… not meat."

He raised his arms. She edged back, alarmed.

"You said that. Okay, what kind of not-meat is it."

"You are not angry?"

"No," he said slowly, fighting the urge to shout. "I'm not angry."

"You sound angry."

"God dammit, why won't you answer a simple question?"

She continued to sit, still, on the end of the bed. At first he thought she was going to cry, but after a while she composed herself.

"It's seaweed. Well, not quite seaweed but something similar. Our special recipe."

"And the potatoes?"

"They're seaweed too. A different kind, obviously."

"Obviously." He tried not to think about why he was eating different varieties of not-quite seaweed being made up to look like not-quite meat and potatoes, but his mouth had other ideas.

"Why aren't you serving real meat and potatoes?"

"Because we don't have any on board. I was assured you would find the food nutritionally satisfying."

"On board?"

She looked alarmed. He realised she'd said more than she was supposed to. He relaxed and changed the subject.

"Say, any chance of getting a TV in here?"

She relaxed too. "A television might be difficult. I might be able to find a film viewer though."

"That would be good."

She returned later wheeling a small screen in on a large trolley. The screen looked like a TV but there were no obvious controls.

"You decide what kind of thing you want to see and it brings up some choices on screen, see?" A menu appeared, she looked to make a decision, a cursor scrolled down until it hit the line she wanted and a film started.

"Sands of Iwo Jima. You're a male, yes? Then you like war films."

"I'm a male, yes." He scratched his head. "And I can do this?"

"Try it."

And he did. He recalled the menu, though he had no idea how. Then he thought of the kind of film he really wanted to see and scrolled down the list until he got to the right one.

"But it's not a war film."

"Right. It's much better than that. Romantic comedy always does it for me. This one's a classic. Man falls in love with a mermaid, or a mermaid falls in love with a man. I forget which. You seen it?"

She shook her head.

"You want to see it?"

"With you?"

"Uhuh."

She smiled. "I'd like that."

The light dimmed and the screen grew larger, though he wasn't sure how that was possible. Deep, cinema quality sound filled the room from unseen speakers.

He's seen the film before, so his mind wandered. But she was completely attentive. After it had finished the lights came back up and she leaned back clapping her hands excitedly.

"That was fun!"

"Told you."

"I've never seen anything like this before."

"Figures."

"You're making fun of me." She looked away.

He could hear the sound of his breathing. He couldn't hear hers. "How long am I going to be here?"

She turned to him, no longer smiling. "I can't answer that."

Next morning the glass stem vase contained a yellow rose. The light was blinding and he wondered how he had managed to sleep with it so bright. He had an idea. He concentrated on bringing the light levels down. And the lights dimmed. Encouraged, he concentrated on bacon and eggs. If he was right about the time – and he had no way of telling – a meal would arrive soon.

She brought his bacon and eggs a short while later.

"This isn't really bacon and eggs," he said, more by way of statement than question.

"Would you believe me if I said it was seaweed?"

"I'd believe anything you tell me," he said, though a mouthful of not-eggs. "Toast was a nice touch. I forgot about toast."

"Your subconscious remembered."

"Yeah. Now how does that work, exactly?"

"Exactly?" she took a deep breath. And for ten minutes he didn't understand a single word she said. He resolved to keep his questions short and simple.

"So I can change the colour scheme?" he said, hoping she'd covered that.

"Weren't you listening? No, you can't. But you can change the way the light refracts."

"Different wavelengths, different colours. Like putting a coloured lens over the bulb." He thought green with a touch of blue, just on the left hand wall. The dazzling white toned down gently to a pastel turquoise.

"That's better. I don't need sunglasses anymore."

"Sunglasses?"

"To keep out the light." He could see she still looked blank. "Never mind – not as funny if you have to explain it."

He experimented with the colours once she had left him. After a while he got bored and the room became white again. As he fell asleep he wondered if it would be pleasant to have pictures on the walls.

When he woke there was a scene from his childhood in a large frame on the wall next to the door. It looked as if it had been painted. It was a good picture, lifelike without being photographic. He got out of bed and looked at it closely. It showed him on a beach rushing towards the water. He was ten years old and his blonde hair was swept back in a style he had envied in others, but his parents had never let him have. They were in the picture too. His father had his arm round his mother, as if the divorce had never happened.

He turned. On the opposite wall was a picture of a man crossing the finishing line at the Olympics and, improbably, he was the man.

He closed his eyes and returned to the bed and sat, rocking gently. When he opened them again the pictures were gone.

"You didn't like the paintings?"

He hesitated, not wanting to seem ungrateful.

"Things didn't work out that way."

"They were how you wanted things to be."

"But not what they were. And I don't want to be reminded of that."

She did not respond, except to tilt her head slightly to the left.

"Am I well?" he asked.

"Yes."

"Then I'd like to go home."

"No."

"You can't keep me here, you know." He tried to remain calm.

She remained impassive. "You're a long way from home."

He felt his anger rising. "What do you want from me?"

She didn't reply at first, but broke away from his gaze, fiddling idly with the sheet at the end of his bed. He thought he saw some hesitation, as if she wanted to say more.

"You are very interesting to us," she said, eventually.

"Me? I'm just an ordinary guy."

"To us you are extraordinary."

He moved over to the end of the bed and grabbed her harshly by the shoulders. "Why are you doing this? Tell me!"

She pulled away. "Because we must," she said, as the door opened and she walked through.

He lay back on the bed and closed his eyes until his heart rate slowed and his breathing became more regular. His anger subsided, to be replaced by a strong desire for understanding. He thought of the woman, and he was surprised to find this relaxed him further. Then he thought of breakfast and breakfast appeared.

He remained alone for the rest of the day. It may not have been a day, because he had no way of telling the time. But on the table, next to the glass stem vase with its pink rose, was a pencil and a notepad. With nothing else to do he wrote, randomly at first, but with increasing inquiry. Where was he? Why was he there? What did the woman want with him? Why had he been kidnapped? Was he going to die?

"We are all going to die sometime," she said when he asked her later. "May I see that?"

"You don't know what's on it already?"

She looked up at him and smiled. "Humour me."

So he passed her the notepad. On it he'd written down anything which could have explained his situation. He had listed a number of alternatives, ranging from lying in a coma after his car accident through to being part of a Government experiment testing out strange new mind altering drugs.

"You think you've been kidnapped by your own government?"

"You read about that sort of the thing all the time. I'm right, aren't I. What are you? Homeland Security? CIA? British Intelligence? You sound British."

"I'm not British."

"You're not from New Jersey, that's for sure. So don't tell me then. I don't care."

She hesitated for a few seconds. "You're on a spaceship. In orbit."

He stared at her. "You're kidding me."

"No."

He should have guessed. The steady thrumming vibration, night and day, the strange technology. The overall weirdness. He made an effort to appear calm.

"How did I get here?"

"We brought you here. Don't worry. You're safe."

He threw his hands in the air, exasperated. He found he had so many questions he did not know what to say. He suspected he would not get a straight answer to any of them. She continued to look at him. Then she left.

When she came back he was calmer. She was carrying an apple.

"Is that a real apple?" he asked.

"Yes," she said. "We grew it up here. We're quite proud of it. Most of the Earth crops we try to grow don't seem to thrive."

"But apple trees take years to grow."

"We've been here for some time." She leaned over and handed it to him. As she did so, his hand brushed hers. It was cold to the touch.

"Thank you," he said.

"You're welcome," she replied. "Would you like to know more about us?"

"If you're ready to tell me."

She nodded. "We think you're ready to listen now." She waited as he took a bite out of the apple. It was good. "We're from a planet about one hundred light years from here. I mean, from Earth. We're in orbit around Earth.

We're a survey mission. We're looking for intelligent species we can join with."

"Join with?"

"It's complicated. But essentially we believe we can only grow as a species by embracing other cultures."

"Like an alliance?"

"In a way."

"Then why didn't you declare yourselves? Why kidnap me?"

She sighed. "It doesn't work like that. We need to study you, to see who you are, and how you would react."

"Well maybe we don't want to be studied!" he said, raising his voice. But he wasn't really angry anymore, just curious.

She turned her head to one side again. "May I ask you a question?"

He nodded, noticing that her hair had begun to tumble across her face. She noticed it too, and swept it back with her hand. He was surprised at how stimulating that was.

"Would you tell us – me – all about yourself?"

He laughed. "Why not? I've got nothing better to do." And he did. He told her about growing up with his father and crying every Christmas when he got the phone call from his mother ringing from Wisconsin, or Hawaii, or Las Vegas, or wherever else her latest boyfriend had taken her to. He told her about college and the army, of work, marriage, sport, of all the successes and all the failures. He told her about sunsets and sunrises, of contentment and frustration, of love and of fear. And when he was finished and he could think of nothing else to say, she reached across and took him by the hand.

"Thank you." She said.

"You're welcome," he replied. And he kissed her on the cheek, not caring that she was cold to the touch.

He was working out on a running machine the next day when she came to visit. He had noticed he was getting flabby and the room had provided workout equipment for him. He was grateful for the distraction of not having to think.

He smiled as she came in and apologised for being so sweaty.

"Are you ready to talk some more?" she said.

"You think we could go somewhere else? I mean, this room is great but it gets boring looking at the same four walls."

She hesitated. "That might be difficult."

He shrugged, and decided not to press the point. "Here, then."

They sat. She was a little closer to him than before.

"Tell me something about you," he said.

"Me? I'm not important."

"Yes you are."

She seemed to be blushing, even though her skin remained porcelain white. "Are you comfortable here?" she said.

"Don't change the subject."

"I want to see another film."

"Don't get to the movies too often?"

"I like to see your reaction. Did you know you were crying a little last time?" she said.

"Me? Dust in my eye, that's all."

"There is no dust in here."

So they watched another film. Then another, pausing only for her to bring him some popcorn when he asked for it. It was good popcorn but when he offered her some she declined politely.

"You didn't cry that time," she said, over the closing credits.

They had been watching a science fiction film. Aliens had landed on Earth and were pretending to be friendly. It had made him feel uncomfortable. This time he had watched her reaction. She had not been smiling.

"No."

"Do you mind if I ask you something else?" She sat right beside him. He was very aware of her proximity. "Will you kiss me?"

Her lips were cold, and at first they were unmoving. But then she followed his lead and they parted a little. Her eyes were open. He pulled back.

"What was that? More observation? And why are you so cold?"

"Cold?"

"To the touch. Freezing. Get out."

He turned away, disgusted with himself for giving in.

After a long time he fell asleep, dreaming of escape. When he woke she was in the bed with him. She was naked, and so was he.

She kissed him this time, with a studied stiffness that softened as he responded hesitantly, eagerly and, eventually, passionately. She was warm to the touch and as she straddled him he gave himself willingly.

Afterwards he was exhausted. She was nestling with her head on his body, her fingers idly playing with his chest hairs. He was no longer thinking of escape.

"Was that another observation?"

"Yes."

"What did you discover?"

"That I liked it. That I like you."

He pulled himself up and looked at her. She lifted her head and smiled. She was beautiful.

"You aren't cold anymore?"

She grinned. "Calibration error."

He suddenly had a thought. "Is this even your real body?"

She kissed him and rose from the bed, heading for the door.

"For a while. Now sleep. You need to sleep."

He didn't think that would be possible. His mind was filled with questions and an agitated restlessness. And then drowsiness overwhelmed him.

"Why do I sleep so much?" He asked her the next time they were together. The sex was better this time, more practiced. She was a quick learner, and he was an eager teacher.

"Because we need you to. Your dreams are very useful for us. You have a vivid imagination, do you know that?"

"And when I'm awake?"

"Then we get to do this."

As the days passed and her visits became more regular and intense he began to get less curious and found he was more accepting. He still asked about going home, occasionally, but didn't mind so much when she evaded his questions. But he wasn't happy.

She had become very attuned to his moods. "What's making you so restless? You have everything you need here."

"I need more."

"What?" she was angry. He had never seen her angry before. "Do you want to go back to the life you had before, is that it? Is it me?"

He was amused by the very human nature of her anger, and relieved by her passion.

"That's not it." He kissed her. "But you must know by now that we humans *are* restless. We need to move on. And we need have some control over what we do. You won't even let me leave this room." He was tired of being a lab rat.

"Nothing lasts for ever." she said, flatly.

"What do you mean?"

"I mean, I can't stay with you for ever. So we should enjoy this time while we can."

Panic hit him. "I don't want you to go."

She smiled and put the palm of her hand on his cheek. "We have a little time yet."

"And then?"

"I don't know."

The next time he saw her she was standing at the end of his bed. She looked miserable, as if she had been crying, even thought he was pretty sure she couldn't cry. She was fully clothed in her white jacket with the collar up, her white skirt and her white boots. Her skirt was creased from sitting on the end of the bed.

"I've come to say goodbye."

He knew she was going to say that so he had concentrated on making himself indifferent. He found he couldn't.

"This body. I have already stayed in this body longer than was intended."

He had suspected. "It's not your real body?"

"Did you think we would look like you?"

"I didn't want to think."

She attempted a smile. "Nor me. I didn't mean for this to happen."

"I thought this was part of the experiment." He said, coldly.

"That part of the experiment ended a long time ago."

She sat and took his hand. He leaned over and kissed her. She pulled away.

"Don't…"

"Is there anything I can do?" He was concerned.

"Understand. Be supportive. This is difficult for me."

They sat for a while in silence. He took her hand again. She let him.

"Would you like to see what I really look like?"

"No." He knew what she really looked like. Her spirit was in the body next to him. He did not need to know what she had been, or would become.

"I'd like you to."

He nodded, reluctantly. She walked them over to the window. The blind began to raise.

Behind it was a fish tank, and in it were fish. Large, vividly coloured fish swimming apparently aimlessly. As the blind opened, three of them turned and swam over, jostling for position as they peered into the room.

They were breathtaking. Yellows and greens mixed in an iridescent swirl of colour flowing like waves though their fins and down their glistening backs. Their faces were curious and expressive.

"Do you look like this? They're beautiful."

"Thank you. And yes. These are my people."

"Why are they in a tank?"

She laughed. "They're not the ones in the tank. Why do you think you can't walk around the ship?"

He stared at the fish and the fish stared back. "Can I talk to them?"

"We talk to each other using what you would call telepathy. Unfortunately your brain doesn't work that way. Why that should be is one of the things we're trying to find out."

"You can read my dreams though, right?"

"Yes. Something in your mind triggers so many possibilities when you're asleep. I'm here for when you're awake."

"But not for much longer."

"No."

"Close the blind, please." the fish swam away and the blind closed. He had nothing left to say so he turned his back on her. She left. He thought of food but found he could only pick at his meal. He lay with his eyes closed, waiting for sleep.

He was still awake when she crept into the room. "There is a way," she whispered. "If you want it."

"What way?"

"I can't bear not to be with you. We've found a way."

"How?"

"To make the body transfer permanent."

He sat up and grabbed for his white smock, realising that this wasn't a conversation to be had naked. Sensing his mood, she covered herself with his sheet.

"That would be a big sacrifice for you to make," he said. "Your people…"

"It would be a big sacrifice for both of us. I would be with you, forever. There would be no going back for either of us."

"Where would we go?"

"We would be home."

He held out his arms and she came to him. He realised that he loved her. "Are you sure?" he whispered.

"I'm sure."

"Then let's do it."

She kissed him softly. "Thank you," she said. And walked out of the door for the final time.

When he woke his vision was blurred and he could only make out dim shapes. Then his eyes cleared and he looked at the vividly coloured fish eyeing him curiously, treading water inches from his face. She swam over and brushed his side gently with hers. It felt good.

"Hello," she said, inside his head.

"Hello," he said back.

"Welcome home." She flicked her tail and sped off.

And he swam after her, his multi-coloured fins shimmering in the dappled light.

Sideways

Our search led to the middle of the Amazon rainforest, to a clearing surrounded by trees, fringed by vines and accompanied by strident birdsong. My humidity-sodden clothes pulled uncomfortably on my back and I'd long given up the futility of wiping sweat from my face. Gina's exhaustion showed in her every step. Even the company soldiers were quieter than usual, more focused. The air smelt of decay and rebirth and something else, something undefinable. Light struggled to find purchase: we were in deep. Just how deep we were about to discover.

We didn't see it at first, because it was behind a large boulder. But we saw the damage it caused, close up. The clearing must have been a hundred meters across, and it was bare of any living thing.

Gina stepped out into the clearing, put her bag down and whistled. Evans pulled her back into the trees. "There has to be a reason nothing's growing in there. Best we find out before we go in."

He turned to me. "Connor?"

I shrugged and sniffed the air. "Smells okay. More ozone, maybe." I waved my detector at him. "Definitely where the anomaly is. Can't tell much more without more sophisticated instruments."

Evans nodded. "Perimeter sweep, then. No one steps inside." Evans sent Cassie and Davis in opposite directions around the clearing. It wasn't an easy assignment–the thick jungle clogged their route. Each carried machetes, but with barely any space to wield them, progress would be slow and ponderous. The local guide, a skinny, nervous native Brazilian called Tupi glanced first at the team's guns, then their machetes, and tried to make himself inconspicuous. Evans and the other members of his team, an unsmiling Iraq veteran called Pryce and a surly kid with prison tattoos on his neck called Jax, talked quietly out of earshot.

They all acted as though they were still in the military. Maybe they were.

I turned to Gina. "Feel anything?"

"Tickles, maybe." She sat down just inside the clearing and searched in her bag for a cereal bar, winking at me as she drew out her food, unappetisingly crushed by pressure and heat, but still with its gaudy wrapper intact. She broke it in two and handed me half.

"Sorry it's not chocolate, but, y'know." She wiped the sweat from her forehead and took a bite.

Ten minutes later Cassie returned, out of breath.

"What happened to your radio?" asked Evans, barely hiding his exasperation.

"Glitched. Bigger things to tell you about though, boss."

Evans and Cassie stood back, away from the clearing, just out of earshot. Cassie talked in fast, short breathless spurts, but she smiled as she spoke and soon Evans's normal fixed scowl softened too. He beckoned us over.

Cassie had found something she couldn't explain and couldn't describe, at least not in any way that made sense. Not for the first time I wondered at the logic of packing the mission with guns and not brains.

We heard Davis's scream from right across the clearing, accompanied by a blinding white light, an inrush of air and an ear-splitting boom. And then silence.

"What just happened?" said Evans in a crouch, rifle drawn.

I waited for the whiteout in my eyes to disperse and my focus to return before looking down at the shattered remnants of Gina's bag. Nothing remained intact, just traces of anything solid: water bottle, binoculars, crampons and pitons, all disintegrated fragments. The rest was dust.

"Well that explains why nothing's growing in there," I said, taking a step further back into the jungle.

Evans made us retreat another ten feet into the tree cover. I didn't think it necessary, but I wasn't about to argue. Whatever had scorched the clearing had been pretty thorough – no doubt about the smell of ozone too. Evans looked for answers I didn't have, so we edged our way round to the other side of the clearing to where we'd heard Davis scream.

The clearing wasn't a perfect circle. As we reached the point directly opposite our original approach, we came across more scorched land even though we'd kept well away from the edge of the damage. It was as if the scorched area had sent out a proboscis, stabbing the jungle with clinical ferocity.

Half of what used to be Davis lay just outside the new scorched area.

Gina noticed the phenomenon first. The rest of us were preoccupied with Davis's remains, but Gina had wandered off in the direction of the clearing to be sick. "Uh, guys?"

A circle of violently jagged energy swirls lay suspended a foot off the floor, backed by the huge boulder that had blocked our view from the other side. The dull light shifted, red, crimson, magenta, violet, all in crisscrossing patterns. Hardly any sound – only the gentle hiss of displaced air. The scorched proboscis lay directly ahead of it.

The swirls were mesmeric. It took me a while to realise the circle was in fact lens shaped. Looking out or looking in? I shivered, despite the heat. The answer probably didn't matter if it killed us all.

"We retreat," said Evans, leading us to a point beyond the tip of the cleared proboscis. No guarantee the next deadly stab would be in the same place, no confidence it wouldn't be soon. Cassie and Pryce cleared some room with their machetes. and we set up a makeshift camp. I tried to get through to base with my sat-phone–no surprise it didn't work. The ozone suggested electrical saturation: no way of telling without instruments I didn't have.

Without the Geiger counter I couldn't even test for radiation. We could already be dead and not know it.

"We should go back," I said.

Evans shook his head. "This is what we're here for."

"But Davis is dead."

"Nothing he didn't sign up for."

The others had hardly talked since we found Davis but I could see them glancing at each other, their masks beginning to crack.

I found Evan's matter-of-fact insensitivity alarming. I'd barely met him, but had been fighting my sense of intimidation from the start. The Company decided we needed support going into the jungle and I hadn't disagreed. But I'd expected local guides, not Company mercs. Before Davis I could fool myself that this was just science, tracking down a mystery energy reading in the middle of sweaty, fetid nowhere. But now it felt like a military expedition, and I wasn't ashamed to feel out of my depth.

Gina and I tried arguing, but Evans wasn't listening. So I set up cameras facing the lens and spent an uneasy night in a rain-soaked tent sleeplessly waiting for the next deadly energy surge.

It came the next morning. We'd just finished breakfast; pouches of what I assumed were army rations heated over an expertly made makeshift fire. The flash seared the proboscis first, then the clearing. Trees shielded us from the worst of the light, but we'd learned from the first time. Despite the dull forest half-light, we all wore protective lenses.

"Same entry point," said Gina, pointing to the area speared by the light, which we had to conclude had sprung directly from the lens.

The cameras yielded nothing useful, just a blight light quickly fading. So I fitted darkened lenses and changed the exposure parameters for the next time. The second flash had been eight hours and twenty minutes after the first. We waited for the third.

Eight hours and twenty minutes later we knew the flashes were regular.

The cameras caught more detail the second time. The energy from the lens brightened, losing its dull colouring and sharpening to an intense white, before pushing out into the forest. Seconds later, the lens flooded the clearing with swirling bright reds and blues and yellows, scouring everything in its path. A bird, foolish enough to fly through the clearing, vaporised instantly, its death squawk lost amid the accompanying boom.

"Why are we still here?"

Evans ignored me. We'd been outside the clearing for five days taking photos and eating increasingly tedious military rations. The pretence that I was in charge of a strictly scientific mission had quietly dropped.

"We're waiting for something, aren't we?" Pryce left two days before, no doubt reporting what we'd discovered. Evans stopped me when I tried to go with him, offering no direct explanation but asking me what instruments I'd need.

Not long after Tupi disappeared too. He'd looked like a terrified rabbit from the first moment he spotted the arsenal we were carrying, and it seemed inevitable he'd abandon us as soon as he got the opportunity. Evans shrugged when I asked him and implied that he'd paid him off and let him go. We knew the way back now so we didn't need him. I envied him, probably sipping beer in a taverna back in Manaus and trying to forget about those stupid Americans.

Jax and Cassie hacked down more jungle, enough to house a whole tent village. That was just after I'd rigged a camera on the end of a branch hacked from a nearby tree and thrust it into the lens. I'd expected some resistance, maybe a hard barrier, but the pole slid in easily. I pulled it out intact, but whatever flew around in the energy maelstrom had wiped the camera.

Not all was lost though. The branch was longer than the lens was deep, and it hadn't hit the back of it. The lens led to somewhere.

We'd found it. We'd found our wormhole.

I fought my instinct just to walk through it. The chances of it leading to somewhere temperate with a breathable atmosphere were remote. We'd need more data, protective equipment. And, I suspected, a death wish. So we got on with the rigorous, scientifically important but slightly frustrating tasks of data gathering and observation.

The wormhole had been one of Gina's theories, back when we'd been working at MIT and before the Company had relocated us and made us wear their fancy laminated badges. Something about the small, localised and periodic variations in the Earth's magnetic field the satellite that had first spotted the phenomenon had detected had got her thinking. That and some inexplicable energy spikes.

"Bet we find tachyons" she'd said. Theoretical, never seen. Just like wormholes.

I shared the wormhole hypothesis with my Company bosses, just like the good scientist I am. Then our funding got sharply increased and Evans and his team turned up, just to complicate our planned jungle field trip.

That's when we decided not to say anything about the other strange readings we'd found, one in Siberia, one on the floor of the Atlantic.

Pryce returned with the backup team. Mainly more guys with guns, but there were a couple of scientists there too, unsmiling guys I'd never met. And Sebastian Kolb, the man who was, effectively, the Company. Kolb was a tall man in his thirties with artfully styled long hair and a reputation for wearing jeans and open- necked shirts in meetings. It unnerved his staid competitors. Truth was, it unnerved me, too.

We had a meeting with Kolb and the scientists not long after they arrived. I was warmed by his enthusiasm and would have told him all I knew if Gina hadn't blurted it all out first. He seemed to know how to put her at her ease, talking in a way I wished I could but would never be able. The other scientists said little, occasionally firing across a technical question. By then the clearing was circled with instruments capable of detecting almost anything. I'd been right about the ozone; radiation levels were slightly elevated too, but not to dangerous levels, and oxygen and helium was slightly more prevalent in the atmosphere than normal. Again, not massively so. Either whatever was on the other side of the lens either wasn't venting atmosphere our way or had the same mix of gases we had.

After that we were effectively edged out. The Company scientists took over, telling us firmly but politely they had everything under control. Kolb reminded us we'd signed confidentiality agreements in a way that suggested we'd signed them in blood. I hoped Gina was as uneasy as I was about that.

We'd found a wormhole and the military – government or private, it didn't matter – were going to exploit it. I ran all the likely scenarios I could in my head and I didn't like any of them.

"When do we go home?" I asked Kolb after we'd been confined to our tents for a week.

"We might still need you," he replied.

"I want to go now."

"We might still need you."

"Can we go?"

Kolb walked off without response.

I picked an insect from my scalp and watched Gina do the same, looking at it in disgust before crushing it in her fingers. We shared a tent now, not for anything sexual but huddled together against the increasingly oppressive atmosphere.

"I'm going to suggest we do something foolish." I said.

"If it involves getting out of here, I'm in."

"We have my detector, which we can use as a compass and we have our sat-phones. Neither works now but a mile or so into the jungle we'll be able to track where we are. I think I can get us back to Manaus."

We didn't risk packing, just grabbing a couple of water bottles, the detector and the phone. We headed out before sunrise.

Half an hour in, Gina cried out and stumbled, falling heavily on her back. Light had started to ooze through the trees and our eyes had adjusted, but the terrain was still too dimly lit for us to avoid all the obstacles in our way.

"You okay?"

"Fine." She got up, winced, but carried on clutching her left ankle. "Just bruised I think."

"Need a rest?" I said, torn by the need to make progress and concern for Gina.

We sat and I took a sip of my water. I suggested Gina do the same but she shook her head. The water had to last us all day. She looked around.

"Something over there." She pointed to a large tree, half hidden by vegetation and gloom.

We moved closer. Propped up on the opposite side of the tree, almost out of sight was a man.

Tupi. His throat cut.

Gina cried out, stepped back. Right into Evans.

They made us take Tupi's body back to the camp, right into the clearing. Our approach brought us to the lens side. Its energy spirals had taken on a disapproving, sulphurous whiff. Kolb leaned against a tree and looked at his watch. "Shouldn't be long now."

Cassie and Pryce stood under the protection of the surrounding trees and trained guns on us, forcing us back towards the lens.

"Why?"

Kolb waved airily. "Because I've decided I won't need you after all. And because you'd go back and tell everybody about the wormhole. Where would be the profit in that?"

I wondered why he didn't just shoot us then I remembered to check my own watch. Maybe he would sleep better knowing that we'd been killed by an energy wave and not by his bullets. Maybe he just didn't want to waste ammunition.

Twenty seconds. Then the clearing would be bathed in a pool of cleansing light.

We were right up against the lens now. Beyond it lay almost certain death, but at least I'd know what was on the other side. Do nothing and we'd die for sure.

I grabbed Gina and pushed her through the lens before the soldiers could react.

I jumped, and immediately wished I'd remembered to fill up my lungs. I'd made no assumptions about how long we'd be in the energy maelstrom. Seconds I could manage. Any more and I'd be dead.

I emerged, panting, onto rock in what seemed to be the inside of a cave. Gina crouched hands on knees. gasping for air.

We lay back on the cold stone and laughed.

"You're not going to believe this place," I said.

Gina shivered. "Let me guess. It's very cold".

I stopped at the cave mouth. "I think 'cold' is the least of our worries."

A ledge lay just beyond the cave entrance, barely big enough for the both of us. I'm a meaty six-three but Gina's wiry, so we could just about squeeze on. We had to be careful though because…

"We seem to be halfway up a mountain." She sounded a bit disgusted and frowned at me as though she thought it was my fault the wormhole had dumped us there.

I ignored her. "Or halfway down." I pointed up, hoping I'd been wrong the first time.

No chance. "Ah. There's ground that way too."

"Told you you wouldn't believe it. We're at the mid-point of a cliff face that goes down in both directions. Which is impossible."

"I can't believe you used the word 'impossible' after travelling god knows where in a wormhole using technology that defies the laws of physics."

Snow drifted slowly down – the down below my feet. I peered over the edge and wasn't surprised to see it speed up a few feet down. Above, the snow seemed to float and move gently in a lazy dance before succumbing to gravity and falling upwards. Or downwards. Clearly we weren't quite at the halfway point because there was a definite down to the way my feet were planted on the ledge.

I glanced down. There were clouds, but I could see stubby trees and what appeared to be farmland beyond them. No buildings, though. I looked up. Clouds there too, but mainly snow flurries. The storm seemed thicker, obscuring most of the sky-ground. It might have been my imagination but I thought I saw a city. Maybe just light reflecting off a river.

Where did the snow come from? There was no sky, only ground and more ground. Sideways, probably. I peered out, though at a distance the snow was thick and I couldn't really see much. Was that 'down' too?

"It's artificial. All of it. Some kind of hollowed out thing and we're near the centre."

"Gravity at the spinning edge, weightlessness at the middle. That would make sense if we weren't almost in the middle and we didn't weigh what we normally do."

"A bit lighter, maybe." I was fooling myself. If I'd had time I'd have come up with another theory, but we had to move. "We need to find another site quickly. Evans won't take long to work out what we're doing."

"Yeah but which way?"

I'd already decided to trust my feet on that one and not worry about the other bit of ground in what should have been the sky. But we had another problem. "That way," I said, indicating the cliff face below us.

"How?"

We had no rope. And the drop was sheer and steep. Worse, if gravity was close to earth-normal now, further down the gravity would crush us. But we had to get away from the mouth of the wormhole before my scanner could detect the next one – and before Evans could catch us.

Wind forced the snow into a flurry, pushing at our faces in a cold caress. "Up, then, until it stops being up." The cliff face bent inwards just above us, cracked and worn. Our view from the ledge was limited, but there seemed to be handholds.

Reluctantly, Gina started to climb. I held back, listening for sounds from the wormhole. Apart from the familiar static crackle, like a distant untuned radio, there was nothing.

Ten feet above, Gina gestured, beckoning me on. "Getting easier. Lighter."

I could hear something now. Voices, in the static maybe. Too quiet to be sure. I started to climb.

"Hold on!"

I stopped, hoping I was wrong about the voices.

"There's something up here." Gina had reached the zero-gravity level and floated, surrounded by suspended snowflakes. They floated towards her, as if attracted to her presence. Her warmth left her in icy breaths. She pointed at something in the distance, but the movement pushed her down the cliff face, closer to where gravity would begin to kick in. Panicked, she grabbed the cliff wall to steady herself.

I could hear them now, squawking. Birds; maybe, or reptiles. Flying over to us. Or floating. "They're gliding in the zero-g."

"They've got teeth, too. And claws."

"Something here, too," I said, trying not to sound too alarmed. But there was no doubting it now: the unmistakable sounds of footsteps and muffled conversation coming from the cave.

I sped up, grasping at rock and missing my footing. I slipped, grabbed hold and started again. Our pursuers emerged, almost at the ledge below us. I tried to meld into the rock, hoping I wouldn't be noticed.

"Connor! You here?"

Evans. I knew Kolb wouldn't risk loose ends. He'd want us dead, just in case the wormhole hadn't killed us. Just in case we found a way back. There was crude science here too; Evans was a test subject Kolb could control. And if he didn't come back? No doubt Evans was as expendable as we were.

I risked a glance below. He wore a full-face mask which made him look like a horror show grotesquery.

Two others emerged. Cassie I guessed, from her bulk, then Jax.

A squawk, from above. Evans reacted. "What th…?"

They all looked up, but at the ground, not at me. "What the hell is this?" said Cassie.

"Gravity's all weird." Evans wasn't showing his usual cockiness. "Artificial habitat, maybe. All built in a hollow sphere, or tube or something. The spin gives gravity on the inner surface, and that's where people would be if there were any." He laughed. "Hey, Connor, you know I can see you, right?"

Cassie pointed her pistol and fired. The bullet zipped past my left shoulder, breaking off rock fragments that flew upwards and continued flying.

That and pumping adrenaline gave me the idea. If the rock could fly on upward, then maybe so could I. Was I close enough to the zero-g? I had little choice. I pushed against the rock and jumped.

The second bullet narrowly whipped past my shoulder, but by then I was off the cliff face, momentum carrying me ten, fifteen feet in the increasingly low gravity. Not enough, because I could feel the ground pulling me back.

Gina grabbed me by the arm and yanked me up, and then I really was floating, free from up and down. I wasn't still though: the storm grabbed me, pulled me from side to side in a dizzying dance of whirls and flurries.

More bullets, strafing the air.

"We've got to move," Gina dragged me and pushed against the cliff simultaneously.

"Where?"

"Sideways." We let the storm take us, gradually slowing with the blizzard shirted from our backs to our faces. Then the wind kicked in behind us, and we gathered pace.

Behind us, more shots, though they weren't firing at us anymore. I turned to see whatever had been squawking bearing down on the ledge. They sounded like reptiles from a Jurassic nightmare. The blizzard made them fuzzily indistinct, but there was no mistaking the menace in the way they flew towards Evans' mercs. The noise attracted them: clearly they'd never learned to fear bullets.

The reptiles reached the ledge. There were four of them. The first one jerked back, hit, and flew off, until caught by gravity and pulled bellow. I watched it turn and start to rise, but its injured left wing wasn't flapping properly. It struggled, but the gravity caught it. Its screech took on a panicked intensity as its slow descent turned into a steady fall, then, suddenly, all efforts to escape its fate ended in futility and it plunged straight down into the abyss.

The remaining reptiles pulled away, screeching in alarm. Not quickly enough for one, which twitched and fell. Our pursuers fired in a panicked frenzy now though. One of the reptiles surged forward, slashed, and sent someone tumbling over the cliff edge.

"What the hell…?" cried Cassie.

"Just shoot it," said Evans.

Jax, then. I never liked him much, and he was trying to kill me, but suddenly any appeal this place may have had faded.

Rifles cracked and the third of the reptiles fell away and the last, finally realizing what was happening, flew off. Once again, the only sounds were the alien songs of the wind and the snow.

I drifted away from the cliff, now barely within pistol range. They had rifles though, but it would be a while before they turned their attention back to me.

Something nudged my leg: Gina. She pulled herself towards me and clasped me in an awkward embrace.

"No ideas, Connor. This is just to stop you floating off."

I liked Gina, because she was rude and independent, but after two weeks in the jungle she smelled like a hippo and had about as much appeal. I was sure the feeling was mutual. She let go and tied something to my belt, then floated a couple of feet away. We were tethered.

"Plan?" I said.

"And here's me thinking you were in charge of this mission."

"Well, obviously we have to get off this habitat before we're either shot, frozen or crushed. And we can't go back, because Evans is in the way and Kolb will be waiting for us." I pulled my detector from my pocket. It wasn't much more than a glorified compass – and this place, wherever it was, had no magnetic field.

I was expecting more wormholes. Three holes on Earth – why not three somewhere else? Three made sense. That was the smallest number you'd need for a network – otherwise you'd just have a string of holes stretching like a necklace with only one way in or out. Three holes opened up an infinity of possibility. Gina scoffed at that because it implied there was something deliberate about the wormhole, but then she didn't read much science-fiction. Me? I knew instinctively there was nothing natural about the phenomenon. Breathable atmosphere here confirmed it. Random, and we'd be breathing raw space or the inside of a star.

The wormholes generated their own magnetic fields, so in the absence of a magnetic field on the habitat the wormholes should shine like beacons, which would make detecting them even easier. The effect was most intense following the energy bursts, but the Amazon hole had shown minor distortions throughout.

The screen indicated the wormhole behind us, but that was all it showed. "We should be far enough away for the other ones to show by now."

"Maybe there aren't any others."

"Trust me, there are more."

"Then where are they, then?"

I glanced back. Behind us, the cliff rose clear to the sky and the ground, an impenetrable wall slicing this world in two. I turned. Ahead of us was nothing.

"That way," I said, pointing at the void.

Gina nodded. "No way of telling, so no harm in trying."

"Exactly. And down or up are probably painful ways to die."

The winds whipped up by the storm gave us a clear means of propulsion, though they were savage and unpredictable and had the deadly potential to push us clear of the zero-g area. Fortunately, they seemed to be forcing us closer to the equilibrium, in an area which seemed deeper than I'd dared hope. Lack of gravity had an odd effect on the wind, too, and as we got closer to what I took to be the habitat's central point it was apparent that it was creating a storm vortex, with a calm area within.

Wings flapped in the corner of my vision and then we were surrounded by reptiles. Up close they were horror show re-imaginings of flying lizards – pterodactyls, or their grim ugly cousins. Sickeningly large rows of teeth marked them out as carnivores, while rows of sharp encrustations on their heads left no doubt that they were frighteningly alien. They were much bigger that I'd thought earlier too –

twice our size and more. I grabbed Gina's arm and saw my alarm mirrored in her face. I waited for the killer blow.

But it never came. The reptiles floated a few feet away from us. We were totally surrounded from all angles and in three dimensions, alone in a sphere of teeth and talons.

"What are they waiting for?" said Gina.

"They're curious. Don't know what to make of us."

"What if "food" is what they make of us?"

"Somehow I don't think we look like food to them."

"That's what I like about you, Connor. Optimism to the point of stupidity."

But I was right. The closest of the reptiles prodded me a couple of times and they seemed puzzled by Gina's long hair which floated randomly in the absence of gravity, but they didn't seem about to tear us apart.

And then a rifle shot, from the direction of the cliff.

The cry from the reptiles was deafening. Another shot, and they started to speed past in the opposite direction, buffeting us as they rushed past. We were forgotten now, at least by the flying creatures.

Evans and Cassie, though, were an entirely different proposition. Without the reptiles to shield us, we would be in full view – and we were well within rifle range.

Instinctively, I grabbed the leg of the last reptile to speed off past me. Tethered, Gina's body jerked behind me until she righted herself and glowered. The reptile turned and cried but then spotted Evans and his rifle, turned again and sped away, clearly deciding to ignore us, at least for the present. We slowly eased ourselves up until we hung below its chest cavity, our weight dissipated by the zero-g.

"This is your plan?" said Gina as a shot flew past her head.

"You have a better one?"

I expected the reptiles to stop, but after a while it became obvious they weren't going to. The reptile carrying us gave up on trying to kick us away and we settled back to enjoy the flight. Away from the cliff the storm began to abate but that didn't slow the reptile's progress: if anything, they got quicker, still finding wind for propulsion but also riding on thermal currents, using the habitat's bizarre atmospheric conditions for the energy they needed to drive them forwards. I could make out features above and below us, to left and right, too: forests and fields, rivers and roads. Buildings as well, mainly in small settlements and isolated structures. I'd been right about the city, too: one of three I saw as we sped past. They were flat, spread thin on the ground, levelled by crushing gravity.

No clue who lived there though, besides gravity's demand that they be squat and strong and I wondered if perhaps it was deserted. If we had more time I would have liked to have found out.

Something else became obvious too, after a while. Gina worked it out first.

"This isn't a sphere, is it? It's a tube."

That made sense. It explained the gravity on the inner surface, presumably caused by a ferocious spin, and the weightlessness at the centre. It must be big, though, because the end wasn't visible at all.

Then my tracing device bleeped and I stared at it, alarmed.

"Down there," I said pointing at a free-flowing river which seemed to meander both below and above our heads. I could see it now, pulsing gently on an island at the river's widest point. The second wormhole.

"Forget it," said Gina. "The fall will kill us."

"Then we have to see this journey out." My teeth chattered. Fear, momentum and my body suit had kept the chill at bay but now the flight had settled into routine doubt – and cold – crept in. Behind us I could no longer see the cliff wall. We flew through a narrow channel with deadly land all around us but nothing, not even a horizon, up ahead. And still the reptiles flew on.

I relaxed as I realised they weren't just flying away from Evans and Cassie. They had a destination in mind, and soon it became clear what that was. The storm started to pick up again, or rather a different storm, up ahead. And beyond it, another cliff wall.

That was their destination: the only other land at zero-g. The reptiles had been scared off from the cliff we'd arrived at, so they were off to the only other place they knew – the other end of the cylinder.

I knew we were in the right place. The tracer glowed faintly, showing the location of the third wormhole.

As they approached the reptiles slowed and started to whirl in formation. One by one they dropped to the cliff wall, where they were greeted by cries and squawks – younger reptiles, welcoming home their parents.

I could see the wormhole now, tantalisingly out of reach. I'd hoped that as our reptile got closer we could let go and let our momentum carry us through. But we were too late – the reptiles were circling now: if we let go we'd veer off into gravity.

Then we were upside down. And we were falling.

The air was full of young reptiles, all rushing to meet us.

Then I realised why the reptiles had been so willing to let us catch a ride.

I had no intention of being food for young flying monsters. I kicked at the first one, connected, and started to fall. I pirouetted, kicked again, each time making sure I nudged ever closer to Gina. I glanced sideways. Gina used the crowd of small reptiles surrounding her to slow our descent. No longer falling, but in deadly danger. Something nicked me on the back of the neck. I turned, snarling, and grabbed its beak, forcing it closed. I prayed it had a jaw like an alligator, deadly snapping closed but weak opening.

My grip held. I twisted, twisted again and tore. The bird renewed its efforts but it couldn't break loose. I swung it, then released. Startled, it fell back on the rocks, hitting with a bone crushing thud. It gave off an anguished cry and dropped away, heading for gravity.

The immediate threat was gone. But I had company, Lots of company.

The adults had left the young to it, when they thought we were just helpless meat. Now they knew better. The skies seethed, noisy, crowded and deadly.

A massive reptile screeched in. I covered my eyes, waiting for the killing blow. But it carried me, instead, ever closer to the cliff. For a second I saw the wormhole then my captor veered away, heading for a clutch of young. I twisted, though its grip was strong. I bashed its left claw with my fist, once, earning a screeching, twice, causing the monster to speed up and three times, forcing it to release me crashing against the cliff. Pain shook through me. Two young approached from the left and I prepared to die. Ahead I saw Gina in a similar battle with two large adults. Each snapped at an arm, each steadily less deterred by her kicks and snarls.

And then the sky exploded.

A lancing bolt thrust out, impaling one of the reptiles attacking Gina. Then a pulse of energy radiated outwards, sending the reptile birds squawking in all directions.

They'd regroup, so there wasn't much time. Gina kicked against the dead lizard and floated towards me. I reached out, grabbed her and started the precarious climb downwards to the wormhole, every moment expecting the rip of claws and talons.

But the reptiles kept their distance, not daring enter the perimeter of the wormhole's intermittent energy field. Now all we had to deal with was the returning pull of gravity.

There was a ledge here too. With far less grace than I would have liked, we fell onto it.

I looked around. In front of the lens was a stone with worn carvings. Pinpoints, each connected to others by three lines. A map! I peered to make out details but the violence of frequent energy bursts had obviously taken its toll. Reluctantly, I abandoned the stone and headed for the wormhole.

"Let's hope the next place is more normal," said Gina as we jumped through.

An eternity later we fell through the crackling energy matrix onto soft sand under a blazing, blood-red sun. Desert all around, but in the distance tall towers gleamed crimson. I exchanged a silent glance with Gina and we headed off to the alien city, no closer to normal, but every step closer to home.

Mad Panic, Flying Paper and Philosopher Cats

"What's going to happen at the end of the world, Billy?"

Billy stared long and hard at Slim. "Nothing's going to happen. Nothing that we'd know about, anyhow. It'll be the end."

"But how will we know it's the end if we don't know what's going to happen?"

Billy watched Slim's chins wobble in harmony as he blurted out his anxieties.

"You won't, Slim. You just won't be there any more. Nothing will."

Slim shook his head hard. "Doesn't make any sense. I'm always here."

Billy was a man of infinite patience and he tested it daily in his conversations with Slim, whose enthusiasm seemed to be in inverse proportion to his IQ. He sighed. "Slim, when the end comes everything will stop. I'll be gone, you'll be gone. We won't be around to see what's going on any more. But we won't miss anything. There'll be nothing to miss."

Slim looked thoughtful, then grabbed Billy by the arms. "Maybe we could ask Matty."

"Slim, Matty's a cat. You can ask him if he wants stroking, but you can't ask him complicated stuff about the end of the world."

"I get more sense out of Matty than most people."

"Yeah, I know what you mean. All he wants to do is eat, sleep and shit. Got his life priorities right."

"Let's go ask him."

So they went to front room of the Big Barge Inn where Matty stood in front of them, stretched out on his front legs and purring.

"End of the world, Matty. What's gonna happen?" asked Slim. Matty responded by rubbing his body against Slim's left leg. "C'mon Matty, it's important."

"What's important, Slim?" came a sweet voice from the doorway. Billy turned to see Darleen in silhouette, hips angled provocatively. Darleen ran the Big Barge, even though she was only the owner's daughter and had no official role there.

"He's asking Matty what's going to happen at the end of the world. Matty's not exactly forthcoming with the answer. I guess that's because he's a cat," said Billy.

Slim squatted on his massive haunches and stroked Matty under the chin. They huddled in what looked like silent deep conversation. Billy decided to leave them to it and headed for Darleen's more obvious charms.

She fixed him a whiskey and he took in the scenery. Usual mix of drunks and furtive couples, working up the courage to ask for a room. The Big Barge was a no questions asked kind of place, which didn't endear it to the local church but which went down well with the bank manager. The lighting was too dim for Billy's taste. He preferred some sunshine with his daylight hours but he could see it helped keep things discreet. Every town needed a Big Barge Inn and Greenville, North Carolina, was no different.

"Keepin' it together Darleen?"

Darleen shrugged. "You know. We open. People come. We close. World goes on."

"Frankie?"

"So long as Pop's got a bottle in his hand he's a happy man. And since Mom left that's all he's got."

Billy took a silent swig.

"But it's okay. Really." Darleen didn't even try to sound convincing. Billy thought about pursuing it but realised he hadn't got the energy. Besides, Darleen could get complicated.

"You know why Slim wants to know about the end of the world, Billy?"

"Search me. Seems to think the cat can talk too. Poor kid's simpler than I thought."

"He's sharper than he looks."

"Darleen, he's talking to the cat."

"Don't knock the cat, Billy. He's sharper than he looks too."

Billy chuckled. "Sounds like you're in on it. Okay, Darleen, tell me all about the end of the world."

"You must have seen the news."

"Nursing a hangover, Darleen. No time for the news."

Darleen poured another glass. "No secret that the bees are all dying, Billy. Or that it's hotter than hell in the summer. Or that the Chinese are beating us at baseball these days."

"You made that last one up, didn't you?"

"Had to check you were still listening."

"So the world's changing. The world always changes. Otherwise we wouldn't have the internet and Barack Obama would still be president."

"Yeah but now the fish are dying."

"So stop fishing. You got any more of that whiskey?"

"I'm saving it for my paying customers, Billy."

Billy took the hint and pulled out a roll of notes.

"Anyway this has nothing to do with the fish." Darleen took Billy's money and stuffed it down her bra. "It turns out that the world's ending next Tuesday. Sometime around three fifteen."

"Eastern Standard?"

"Greenwich Mean."

"And how do you know all this?" Billy was puzzled.

"It's on the flyers."

"Notices stuck on disused buildings by cranks? Must be true then."

"No, the <u>flyers</u>. Notices hovering eighteen inches from people's faces. In the air. Not on strings. Inexplicably defying gravity."

Billy thought Darleen was talking nonsense. "Saying?"

"You've been bad. The day is coming. Don't make plans for next Wednesday. Remember to feed the cat."

"They say just that?"

"Well, obviously I'm paraphrasing. The bit about the cat was in there though."

"Hence Slim's interest in the philosophical musings of Matty, I suppose."

"You going to drink yourself to a stupor or are you going to walk me into town for some lunch? The regular staff can handle the drunks in here."

"Lunch is good." He levered himself off the stool. On the way out Billy waved at Slim who was locked in conversation with the cat. Only the cat looked up.

"Don't you feel guilty about leaving the bar?" said Billy.

"I don't get paid enough to feel guilty. And if the world's going to end next Tuesday I need to take some time off now. Use it or lose it."

Billy grabbed a paper from the reception counter. "Says here it's all a big hoax. They're trying to work out how it's done. Police are raiding most of silicon valley looking for computer geeks with too much time on their hands."

"If it was computer geeks wouldn't they have posted this on the internet?"

Billy tossed the paper in the trash as they headed out into the cool daylight. "Stuff like that's on the internet all the time. Nobody listens any more. Flying paper is much more convincing. But c'mon. If it really is the end of the world, what's the point in telling us about it?"

They ate at the Rib Shack on the corner of Ninth, where they had a good view of the traffic. Billy noticed an unusually large number of cars heading north to the hills, all fully loaded. He ignored the ribs and went for the steak, done rare the French way. Darleen ordered a salad full of unidentifiable green things.

They had to wait for their food. "Sorry," said the waitress. "Not everyone turned up today. All this talk about the end of the world's got folks spooked."

"Still, means you'll get some time off."

The waitress looked at Billy curiously. He noticed she had her name badge, 'Angie', pinned the wrong way round.

"Next Wednesday. If the world ends you won't need to open. Have a lie in. Put your feet up."

Upside-down-Angie flushed and scurried off.

"You're not taking this seriously," said Darleen.

"That's because the sun will come up next Wednesday, as usual, and I'll be hung over, as usual."

"How do you explain the flying flyers then?"

"I don't. I'm just a car mechanic. I leave the unexplained stuff to people who can explain it. Maybe the cat can tell us."

He looked at her full in the face. She had a smile waiting on her lips. "Anyhow, you don't believe it any more than I do. It's just a ploy to get me into bed."

"Well what else are we going to do at the end of the world?" she said, smile breaking out at last.

"Won't work. There's no future in it."

"Spoilsport."

The waitress came over to clear their plates.

"Hey upside-down-Angie?" said Billy. "What do you think about all this end of the world talk?"

"Right now I'm thinkin' it's the only way I'll get any peace around here. You kids done?"

"Coffee, Angie. Black and strong."

"Stop terrorising the staff," said Darleen, after Angie had disappeared into the kitchen.

"Can't help it. I've moved from indifferent to amused on the whole end of the world thing. Anyway, I've started to get interested in Slim's question about what's going to happen. Whether it's next Tuesday or seventeen billion years from now, the end's gonna come. Bang or a whimper?"

"Whimper," said Darleen, folding her arms and slouching back in her seat. "The stars just run out of fuel then everything's black. Maybe the universe contracts into a big black hole and the whole thing starts up again."

"That's not an end, it's a cycle." Billy's brain was beginning to hurt.

"Easier to get your head round than answering the question about what comes next, right after the end."

"The sequel."

"Yeah, but that's billions of years from now, probably. What if the world actually did end next Tuesday?" Darleen started to play with Billy's leg, under the table.

"Well what are the choices?" Billy moved uncomfortably, but he let Darleen's leg continue its journey up his thigh.

"Killer disease. Nuclear war. Aliens. Supernova. Asteroid attack. Mass panic."

"I vote mass panic. I think those flyers are working." Billy looked out of the window to see an argument breaking out between the owners of two heavily packed flat beds which had collided, bringing the intersection to a halt.

"We've got to get out of here." Darleen pulled her leg back and reached for her bag. Billy took out a couple of notes and rose quickly, winking at the harassed waitress on his way out. She ignored him.

"Where to?" said Billy.

"Anywhere but here."

"Stick to the coast then. Because everybody else is heading in the other direction. Panicked people are stupid people and we don't need to be around stupid people."

"Can we use your truck?" said Darleen.

"It's Slim's truck. Only I won't let him drive it on account of, y'know."

"Yeah I know. His complete inability to drive."

"That and his tendency to talk to cats," added Billy.

"Guess he's coming with us then."

"But he's…"

"Stupid, I know. But he's our stupid."

They found Slim at the bar of the Big Barge looking puzzled.

"What did the cat have to say, Slim?" said Billy, slapping him on the back.

"Says I should look after myself, while I still can."

"He said that? What, out loud? Words and everything? Think we can get him on TV?"

Slim slunk back into his seat. "I know you think I'm crazy, Billy. But the cat and me had a good chat. I don't know about using words. I don't think that's how he does it."

"Want to tell us about it on the way? We're going on a trip. Florida. To the beach!"

Slim brightened. "Can the cat come?"

Billy shook his head. "No cats." Then he caught the look on Darleen's face. "Okay okay. The cat can come. But one sight of its claws and it's out the window."

Darleen insisted on driving, even though the truck was a stick shift and she'd never driven one before. Billy sat in the middle of the one long seat, pressed close to Darleen by Slim's giant bulk. The cat purred happily on Slim's lap. They met plenty of cars going the other way but nothing going south.

"Need to stop for some sunglasses, Darleen. Think maybe that's how the world's going to end. Solar flares."

"You starting to believe?"

"I believe that's a gas station over there, which is as good a place as any to get sunglasses."

Darleen pulled in. The place was deserted. They eased themselves out of the truck.

"Door's smashed," said Billy. Darleen held back.

Slim pushed forward. "Maybe they'll have chocolate."

"Hold on Slim. There could be trouble."

But Slim was already at the door. "Looks like the place has been smashed up bad, Billy. The chocolate's all over the floor."

Billy cursed himself for not spending five minutes detouring to get his gun. Fortunately the shop was empty.

Slim dropped to his knees and scrabbled for chocolate bars while the cat purred contentedly round his swollen ankles. Darleen appeared with some designer sunglasses.

"We've got to go," said Billy fishing in his pockets. He produced a twenty and placed it gently in the till.

"You paying for them?" Darleen sounded surprised.

"Sure. You think I'm going to steal them? C'mon."

They hurried back to the truck, with Billy bringing up the rear, looking for trouble. But the place showed no signs of life.

"So what exactly did the cat tell you?" said Darleen, grinding the transmission into second gear.

"He says we're killing all the fish. And cats like fish."

"See? Told you." Darleen looked triumphantly at Billy.

"Let me get this straight. The cats have decided to call time on the world because we're killing all the fish."

"I'm not sure about that, Billy. I think for the cats if all the fish have gone that means it *is* the end of the world."

"They eat chicken. They'll be okay."

"He was a bit hazy about the world ending, Billy. I don't think he'd read the flyers. But he said some nice things about you."

"He did not. I hate cats."

"Said you sneak him food when no-one's looking."

"I do not." Billy noticed Darleen grinning.

"That's not what the cat says. Anyway he mainly asked a bunch of questions back at me. Like 'what is the world'? and 'what is the end?' Oh, and 'what's for dinner?'"

Helpful, thought Billy. Mad panic, flying paper and philosopher cats.

#

They drove on through washed out country drabness, patchy rain deadening the landscape, greying out the colours and misting out the contours of the dusky hills to the right. They just passed the border between the Carolinas when they came across the road block. A truck, a camper van and several SUVs completely closed off the southbound lanes. Two masked men with guns started walking slowly towards them as they pulled to a halt.

"Get out of the vehicle," said the front guy, red scarf tied around his face. Darleen eased herself out of the cabin. The men relaxed a little.

"You need to give us all you've got, miss," said the one, masked with a blue bandana.

Billy cursed again about his lack of firepower. He eased into the driver's seat.

"Are you robbing us?" said Darleen, coquettishly.

Billy fingered the starter.

"Road toll, miss. Money first."

"And then?"

"Special toll."

The men seemed to have forgotten that there were two other people in the cab. Billy started the engine. The men suddenly brought their weapons up, but it was too late. They were too close and Billy was right on top of them. He caught red scarf on the side as blue bandana scrambled out of the way. Darleen grabbed the open truck door and hauled herself in.

"Now what," she gasped, as bullets started flying.

"Now we keep our heads down and hit the gas."

Billy drove at the camper van, figuring it was the lightest and would cause the least damage. But, last second, the van moved and they were through.

"Darleen," asked Billy when things had calmed down a bit. "When the guys back there said 'special toll', how come you just wiggled your hips at them?"

"Were they looking at you at any point during the conversation?"

"No, but…"

"Then that's why I wiggled my hips."

"Yes, but…"

"Do you seriously think they were going to get what they wanted? Really? Worst bunch of would be robbers and rapists I've ever come across."

"You've come across robbers and rapists before?"

"I watch a lot of TV. Anyhow, those guys were amateurs. A taste of things to come maybe. As the end gets closer."

"How many times do I have to say it? There is no end!"

"Doesn't mean we're not going to get closer to it. That's about distance, not time."

"Matty wants to know if there'll be any fish where we're going," said Slim.

"We're going to the coast, Slim. What do you think?"

"I'll tell him you don't know then, Billy."

They got the rest of the way down without any more incidents, though they kept well clear of Jacksonville, on account of the distant gunshots and the dull red glow of the fires that seemed to be setting the whole city alight. Billy kept his eyes on the road and his thoughts to himself. If the military base there had been compromised he didn't want to be anywhere close by, so he sped up.

The highway was mainly deserted, but Billy spied what looked like a pack of dogs staring at them from the side at one point. The cat hunkered down in the footwell.

"You hear about the four minute warning experiment?" said Darleen, breaking the silence. "Small town of about five thousand people out in Arkansas. The authorities co-ordinated an experiment to convince everyone the Russians had launched a nuclear strike and they had four minutes to live. Sirens, TV, radio, the Internet – all carrying the end of the world message. What do you think happened?"

Billy gathered his thoughts. "An awful lot of sex, probably."

"Surprisingly not. Most everybody just got on with their days. There was a big increase in people cleaning their homes, though, and washing their cars. When they asked them afterwards they said they didn't want to die with a dirty house knowing they had time to do something about it. Go figure.

"Anyhow, a significant minority decided that if they were all going to die anyway, then they might as well just hurry things along. Two hundred and fifty murders, including a kid with an Uzi and a grudge in his high school class, and three hundred suicides. Now they know."

"How come I never heard of this experiment?"

"*Because* now they know. And no-one's going to get re-elected after an experiment in which ten percent of the people involved died. But Billy, that was four minutes. Imagine what might have happened in four <u>days</u>?"

Billy gripped tight on the steering wheel.

They reached a seafront place Billy had visited once just north of Boca Raton. The highway was pretty deserted at that point and the hut was shielded from the road by a bluff.

"We'll be safe here."

The place was locked up tight so Billy had to break a window. Fortunately the intruder alarm seemed to be disconnected. Cheapskates probably just put a flashing box up and hoped that would scare folk off, he thought gratefully. Slim made himself right at home and flicked on the TV. Darleen headed for the kitchen, looking for cat food.

"Hey, there are riots in Paris, Billy."

Billy grabbed the remote and turned the volume up. "Other places too, Slim. Looks like the world's going crazy." London was under martial law. Someone tried to firebomb the White House, and rioters and police fought a pitched battle on the Golden Gate Bridge.

"What the hell is going on?" said Darleen, returning from the kitchen with a plate of chicken for the cat.

"Exactly," said Billy. "Don't we get some food too?"

"You want food? At a time like this?"

"I always want food, Darleen. Just because the world is ending doesn't mean I'm not hungry."

"I thought you said the world wasn't ending."

"Does that look like the world you knew?"

"Well, no, but hey – we've still got TV."

At which point the power went down. Darleen stumbled around for a minute or so then returned from the kitchen with some lit candles. They sat in glum silence. After a while Billy went into the kitchen and made some sandwiches. For the first and only time he could remember, Slim refused the proffered plateful. Darleen turned her back. So Billy ate alone. Almost alone, that is, because the cat wasn't fussy.

On Tuesday morning they woke tired and anxious. Slim had his appetite back so he fixed breakfast. Billy closed his eyes and tried to pretend it was last week, before all this madness started.

Darleen looked rumpled. "You seen the time?" she said.

"Yeah, nearly a quarter after ten."

"Which makes it almost three fifteen, Greenwich Mean Time."

"End of the world, then. Time to, you know?"

"Yeah," said Darleen winking. "Time to tidy up." She led the way to the bedroom and closed the door gently.

"With a bang, then, after all." Billy said happily afterwards, alive, with the world still turning, and Darleen's head resting gently on his chest. The sun peeking through the blinds accentuated the colours in Darleen's wild hair. "So what are we going to do now?"

"Only thing we can do under the circumstances. Go shopping." So they headed into Boca Raton. The place was completely deserted. "Where is everyone?" said Darleen, holding Billy's hand.

"I don't like this Billy. I don't like this at all." Slim had Matty pressed tightly to his chest. He'd found him nosing at what he thought at first was a pile of rags, deep into the driftwood by the sea's edge. After that he wasn't going to let him out of his sight.

The door to the drugstore had been smashed open. Billy led the way, gingerly. Inside the place was in disarray and a smell coming from the rear of the store persuaded him not to look too closely. Most of the other shops were the same, except for the bookshop, which was open and intact. Inside an old woman sat behind a counter, reading a copy of Nostradamus' prophecies.

She chuckled. "Says here that he world's not really going to end until the year 3797. I guess I've got time for a cup of tea then."

"You surely have. Mind if we join you?"

"Be glad of the company. Been pretty quiet round here this last few days, since everybody started to go crazy. Once the shooting stopped, most people just stayed indoors with their blinds down."

"And you? Did you believe the world was going to end?"

"Well maybe if I paid any notice to what you see on TV I might have believed it. You seen one of those magic pieces of flying paper yourself? Thought not."

"Maybe it's a self-fulfilling prophecy," Darleen added. "You know, enough people expect something to happen, so it happens."

The old lady chuckled. "That would explain the mushroom clouds out Jacksonville way. End of the old world, that's for sure. And I for one won't miss it."

After they finished their tea the four of them, and the cat, emerged blinking into the scorching Florida sun.

"First day of the new world," said the old woman. "And it's going to be a hot one."

Down at cat level Matty smiled. For the first time in weeks he could smell fish.

Immersion

Jason turned the corner and the city laid itself before him, lolling gracelessly down the hillside and into the valley below. At first glance it seemed the same as when he'd left, thirty years before. But as they moved closer he realised there was something different. It felt quieter than he remembered, but that wasn't it. And then it hit him. The city's soul had gone.

"We walked three days for this?" said Hender.

Jason glanced over at his travelling companion. "Don't be negative."

Hender just grunted in response. Jason didn't really care what he thought. He wished he'd stayed behind at the Refuge but no, his friend scented a great adventure, free from the constraining walls of their slowly disintegrating home. Almost as soon as they waved goodbye, though, he started moaning. Jason stopped listening.

By nightfall they reached the heart of the city, after hours of passing through clean well-kept streets, immaculately serviced by maintenance robots. From time to time they saw lights shining behind drawn curtains, high in the upper stories of old brick tenement blocks and newer chrome and steel apartments. They'd passed through the vastness of the city all day but hadn't seen any people.

They reached a restaurant called Lucy's with light spilling out onto the street. It represented the first real signs of life they'd seen, and strongly appealed to Jason's growing hunger. The place was half full but any noise there stopped as soon as the two of them entered. The barman nodded as they walked over to a circular bar in the middle of the room, and conversation resumed.

"Not seen you here before," said the barman.

"We're from out of town," said Jason.

"*Way* out of town," said Hender.

"Eating?"

Jason nodded, and the barman led them to a table. They ate everything laid in front of them, then they ordered more.

The other diners were mostly middle aged or old, all except a young couple in a table in the dark part of the room, right at the back. They didn't look tired, they looked exhausted.

A woman entered, dressed in a long red cloak. As she walked over she let the hood fall, revealing long curly auburn hair. She glanced at Jason, then sat in the vacant seat between Jason and Hender.

"Mind if I sit here?" Before Jason could answer she called across to the barman, who brought over a bottle of Merlot and three glasses.

"We don't..." Jason started.

She silenced him with a hand on his wrist. "Go on. Live a little." She poured and sat back, sniffing appreciatively. "Most of the vineyards have closed down now, you know. On account of the dwindling numbers of connoisseur drinkers."

"We don't drink," said Hender, wine dripping from the edge of his mouth. "Usually."

"You must think us uncouth. I'm Jason. This is Hender."

"Lucy." She smiled. "Yes, this place is mine. And I think you're charmingly different."

She eased back her red cloak to reveal an expensive dress with pearls round her neck, with the distinctive flash of gold in her ears. "You've dressed up. Were you expecting someone?"

She waved dismissively. "My little idiosyncrasy. It's Saturday night. You're supposed to dress up on Saturday night, right?"

"Where is everybody?" said Jason. The lighting had edged down a notch, and Hender had disappeared somewhere. Another bottle appeared on the table. "Last time I came to this city it was heaving. People everywhere."

"They're still here, mostly. But like everywhere else you, well, you know."

"Pretend I don't know."

"Where did you say you were from?"

Jason waved vaguely out of the window towards the East. "A community in the hills. We've been kind of cut off."

"No tanks?"

"No what?"

"No V worlds?"

"Just farming and prayers."

She laughed. "Should have guessed from the funny clothes. And the fact that you're here at all. So what brings you to the big city?"

Jason gave her the brief version. About the Community and how it had been set up, years before, as a back to basics antidote to the bored listlessness of the robot serviced paradise that the Elders had seen coming. He skipped over the bit about how the Refuge had reached capacity and the elders had placed prohibitions on childbirth. About the hunger, the deprivation and the pointless rules and discipline. About the stupidity of thinking you could cut yourself off from the world and somehow it would be all right.

"It's a little world up there and times are tough. One day I woke up and I said to myself, 'ice cream. I want ice cream.' So here I am."

"Then ice cream we shall have." She laughed. "We do an excellent Rocky Road in here."

The ice cream was even better than he remembered. "So," he said as he licked his spoon. "The tanks. Tell me about them." He was vaguely aware that Hender should have been back by now, but the wine blurred his thinking and the food made him slow.

"Boring. Let's talk some more about farming. You people still grow your own food? Yourselves?"

He could see Hender now, at the table in the back of the room, talking to the young couple. Jason looked more closely at them. They were dishevelled, with lank long hair tied roughly in ponytails. Despite the gloom and the sympathetic candle glow, Jason could see that they were pale, as if denied the sunlight which still peered occasionally through the rain-sodden clouds. "Who are they?"

"Izos. Making a rare excursion back into the real world. Don't see many of them these days."

"Izos?"

"Immersion Zombies." She shook her head in irritation. "Damn. You've got me talking about the tanks after all."

"Does that explain why there are no people around here?"

But instead of replying she sat up, pulled her shawl around her shoulders, and made her way slowly to the door. Then with a smile she nodded gently to Jason and left the restaurant, leaving behind a waft of perfume and the icy blast of the late evening chill.

Hender returned just as Jason finished the bottle. "I've got us a bed for the night." He gestured over to the exhausted couple. "Close, too."

They headed for the seventh floor of a nearby high rise. The couple clung to each other and did their best to avoid eye contact with either Jason or Hender.

"Jason," said Jason as the doors closed.

"Butterfly," one mumbled.

"Drax," said the other one.

"That your real name?" said Jason before he could stop himself. He was tall, certainly, but he slouched in a way which suggested he wasn't used to his own body. "You don't look like a Drax."

"Kevin," he mumbled.

Butterfly scowled. "I didn't know that."

"What I used to be." He turned away. "Before."

The elevator opened into a short, brightly lit corridor. The carpet appeared new, but Jason suspected that was just because not many people walked on it and because the maintenance robots did a good job of keeping the dust at bay. Drax stopped by a dull metal door and pressed his palm against a security pad. They were in.

The blinds were down and the lighting subdued. The apartment had the feel of a recently serviced hotel suite, stripped bare of anything which made a house a home. There were chairs, a table, even a vase, though it didn't look like it had seen flowers in quite some time. A slight smell of ozone mixed with a chemical residue which Jason couldn't quite identify. Half detergent, half... something else.

The girl shuffled over to one of the single large sofa which dominated the open space. Drax sat next to her, leaving Jason and Hender standing awkwardly.

Hender broke the silence. "Say, you guys wouldn't have any coffee would you?"

Drax shook his head and blinked, as if coming out of a trance. "Wha? Oh. Kitchen." he waved at a closed door. "Good idea." He got up, quickly followed by Butterfly and soon Jason could hear percolating sounds and the distinctive comforting smells of a good roast.

"Who are these guys?" said Jason. "They're deathly pale and they have really bad acne. They should use cleanser. Or get out more."

"Yeah, well, I don't think they're used to getting out at all. I get the impression they met each other in one of those virtual worlds. I think this might be the first time they've actually met, in the flesh."

"They don't seem to have much to say to each other."

"They seemed mighty pleased to see me. I guess the alternative to having us around is that they might actually have to talk to each other."

"Where'd you guys meet?" said Hender as Butterfly came in with a tray of coffee.

"Ragnarok," said Drax.

"Ragnarok Five, actually," said Butterfly. "I was attracted to his blue wings."

Drax smiled. "The same shade as hers. It seemed we were meant for each other."

Jason noticed they avoided eye contact. "You spend a lot of time in Ragnarok?"

"All the time," said Butterfly. "Until yesterday."

"*All* the time?"

Drax shrugged. "Couple of years maybe. Spring of '92. There was a heatwave so I closed the blinds."

Not been opened since, thought Jason. "Drax, that was twelve years ago."

"Really?"

"You telling me you've been in Ragnarok for *twelve years* without a break?"

Drax looked pained and took another sip of his coffee. "Don't sound so judgemental, man."

Butterfly leaned forward. "Drax was already there when I joined. He was in charge, actually. Well as far as the game parameters would let him. Ragnarok Five's a benign game."

"Meaning?"

"Meaning the system won't let you screw things up for the other users. So Drax got to rule over one of the Seventeen Kingdoms as long as he kept everybody happy enough to want to stay."

"You didn't stay."

Butterfly started to sob. Drax turned his back. Even Hender seemed uncomfortable.

"Look," said Drax. "This is painful. Maybe we should talk about it tomorrow."

"Or not talk about it at all," said Butterfly.

"Perhaps we should go," said Jason, ignoring the panicked look on Hender's face.

"No!" said Drax and Butterfly together.

So Hender took the couch, and Jason curled up in the corner under a borrowed blanket. He assumed the others discovered a bedroom somewhere.

Jason was still bleary eyed when Hender shoved a cup of coffee in his hand. He took the first sip instinctively.

"Good. Stronger than last night." He nodded in satisfaction. "Where are Kevin and the girl?"

"You mean the people formerly known as Drax and Butterfly? Presumably still finding out whether they like each other in the real world, whatever that is."

Sun shone through the slats in the blinds. Jason checked his watch. "I'm going to check on them." He left Hender trying to work out how to operate the View Wall. He knocked gently at first, but when he got no answer he knocked again, louder this time.

Someone inside was crying.

The door wasn't locked and the handle turned easily. Black drapes covered the window and the only light came from the doorway. The room was crowded; as well as the bed, wardrobe and other furniture a large rectangular box shoved over to one side filled most of the available space. Butterfly leaned against it, slumped to the floor, sobbing.

Jason flicked on a light. "Where's Drax?"

Butterfly gestured over her shoulder, to the rectangular box.

"In there?" Jason walked over and peered in through the glass panelled lid into the box, filled with viscous fluid. And something else: Drax. "What the hell is this?"

They took her to the park mainly to get her out of the apartment, but also because they were hungry and the only food they could find at Drax's was way past its use-by date by several years. It was mid-morning but apart from a solitary jogger and a couple of old women chatting on a bench they didn't see anyone until they reached the auto-café at the northern edge. An old man looked them up and down, waved his coffee cup in greeting and shuffled off, mumbling something inaudible as he left. He wore an old business suit, frayed at the cuffs and collar, too small for him now, but his shirt looked clean and pressed and he wore a tie which might have been new. Keeping his standards up, Jason supposed. Maybe the alternative was giving up.

She stopped crying after she'd finished the second sandwich. "That's the first food I've had since we came out."

"But you were in the restaurant last night," said Jason, helping himself to more coffee.

"Doesn't mean I was eating. I thought I'd forgotten how."

Somewhere a dog howled. Jason tried his best to ignore it. "Tell me about Drax. About the box."

"Box? Oh you mean the tank."

Jason gave his best blank expression.

"You really are from out of town, aren't you? The tank. The V-world Immersion Chamber."

"Look, Butterfly, or whatever you'd like me to call you out here. Last time I was here you accessed V-world with a nifty little wide headpiece. I do remember it getting almost so you couldn't tell you weren't actually in the real world. But I don't remember people closing themselves off in coffins."

"Yeah, well. Progress. The old V-worlds were great, no doubt about it. Or they would have been if you didn't still need to eat or shit. That meant forty-eight hours, tops. Maybe more with a drip and a game nappy. But you know, it's kind of a mood breaker unplugging to deal with your own fetid crap. Not to mention the smell."

"So now you encase yourself in nutrient fluid and you never have to leave the game," Hender said. Jason shot him a glance. "What? Despite appearances I do read stuff you know. There are intelligent nanoparticles in the goo which regulate bodily functions and apply electrical stimulus to the muscles, which is why Butterfly here can walk and talk like a normal person."

Now Butterfly shot him a glance. "I know I look bad to you, but apart from the spots and the whitewash face I'm telling you I feel better than I've ever done out here. I mean, before I hit the tank I was two hundred pounds and getting bigger. Moving to Ragnarok probably saved my life."

"Then why leave?" said Jason.

She sighed. "It was Drax's idea. We were in love, and we wanted sex."

"You can't do that in the game?"

"You can do anything you want in the game, including and especially sex, in all its forms. Subject to the parameters of the particular world you're in of course. Which in Rangnarok means that eight foot tall blue guys with equipment sized to match and three foot nothing flying insects were never going to get it on, not really."

"Hence your brief return to the real world."

"And what a waste of time this has turned out to be."

"So I guess Drax has gone back."

"I think I was a bit of a disappointment to Drax. But that's okay. He was more than a bit of a disappointment to me."

"Are you going to go back too?"

Butterfly laughed, but with no smile behind it. "I think the spell's been broken, don't you think? Anyhow, you can't go back, not to the same place anyway, which is another reason people never leave. Once you leave the system resets you with a new identity. Drax ain't Drax any more."

Lucy, at the bar, sipped a martini. "Hoped you'd be back."

He smiled. "Only place left in town where a real human takes your coat."

"Not quite true. But it's certainly the only one where you'll get a decent cocktail."

Hender and Butterfly went to the table Drax and Butterfly had taken the night before. This time, though, Butterfly studied the menu as if she was actually preparing to order something, and absently picked peanuts from a bowl. She seemed more animated and less dishevelled too.

Lucy gestured in Butterfly's direction. What did you do with the other one?"

"Gone. Back in the tank."

She pursed her lips. "That hateful word again. So I guess you've found out where all the people have gone. Why be bored here when you can be a barbarian king, or a beautiful princess, or a slayer of vampires?"

"Because here is real and there isn't, maybe?"

"Believe me, it can feel pretty real in there. And once they're in, they stay. It's amazing how persuasive a combination of the good life, virtual hard drugs and an entirely rational fear of how fast things are degenerating out here can be."

"So what keeps you out?" asked Jason.

She stirred her drink with a cocktail stick. "Did you know they first designed the tanks to be used in prisons? With the in-game opt-out protocols disabled, just to make life more interesting."

"I would imagine that enabled some pretty extreme forms of punishment."

"Rape, torture, dismemberment, you name it. When you're in there, it's real. And if you can't get out, it might as well be real." She smiled and crossed her legs. "I used to work for V-corp, did I tell you that? I worked on the early V-world models, before the AIs got so damn clever they didn't need us anymore. Then one day I argued with the wrong guy about the morals of zombifying minor criminals and torturing them for ever, so they tanked me. They put me in one of the prison scenarios."

"You mean you got arrested?"

She shook her head. "Nothing so official. They dumped me right on in. No prep no warning no nothing. One minute they were forcing my head into the glop and the next I was crawling on a mountaintop in a blizzard. With no way out."

"So how did you escape?"

"I'll come to that. Those first minutes all I thought about was getting off that damn mountain. I found a cave, fortunately. Otherwise it would have been all over for me."

"Are you saying that if you die in the game you die for real?"

She shook her head. "In the prison worlds, you neither get to die nor leave. If I'd collapsed on that mountaintop I'd have been frozen for ever. Alive, conscious and probably completely mad by now. I got lucky. But then the other prisoners found me."

"And?"

"Don't want to talk about it. Think of your worst nightmare? Not even half way there."

Jason waited for her to continue but her eyes glazed, staring into the distance. When she eventually spoke, she talked quietly. "They pulled me out after a week. Laughed about it. Thought it was all a big game."

"Explains your hatred of the tanks."

"Just gives me a different perspective, that's all."

They ate, then, the four of them, bathed in candle light. Real food, probably grown in one of the underground hydroponics plants that Jason had heard about. It all tasted delicious.

"So, Butterfly, think you'll go back to Ragnarok?" said Lucy.

"Sandra. I'm Sandra now. No wings, see?"

"Thought we'd try one of the other Worlds," said Hender.

"What?" Jason said through a mouthful of food. "'We'?"

"Let's face it, Jason. This place is finished. Everybody's gone. I need to go where the action is."

"Yes," said Butterfly/Sandra, smiling. "And this time I'll be going with someone I actually like on the outside. I think that'll make a difference." Jason noticed they were holding hands.

"Why don't you come with us?" said Hender.

Lucy sighed. "You know that people in the tanks rarely leave, don't you?"

"I did," said Sandra.

"You've been out barely two days and you're going right back in. I hardly think that counts."

"Don't care anyway," said Hender. "I'm done here."

"Yeah, don't be so down on it," said Sandra. "Don't knock it 'til you've tried it."

They ate the rest of the meal in subdued silence. Jason went to the bathroom when they'd finished their coffee. When he got back to the table Hender and Sandra were gone.

Lucy poured herself a glass of wine and, hesitating, topped Jason's up too. "Come. Let me show you something."

They took an AutoTaxi to an industrial estate on the edge of town and pulled up next to a vast grey windowless structure. Lucy led them in through a small side door which Jason could barely see: grey on grey.

They were in a massive open hangar. They climbed a rampway to a platform suspended maybe twenty feet above the floor where they could see the whole floor area. The warehouse was full, floor to ceiling, with rectangular boxes stacked in shelves and in neat, seemingly endless rows. Immersion tanks. Thousands of them.

"Impressive, eh?" said Lucy. "Didn't take long for the tanks to move from the prisons to the general population. Back then we still had an economy that used money, before we could leave everything to the androids and the AI. At first it was the hardcore gamers and a few curious kids. Then they became fashionable as a kind of retirement community. A place in the sun at a fraction of the cost, and, more importantly, a place where you never seem to get old, even though your physical body might be falling apart.

"That was maybe twenty years ago, just about the time the wars ended. That meant a lot of young people coming home without work to do. It didn't take the Government long to work out it was cheaper to offer free tanking than to provide social security to millions of the unemployed. So they hit the tanks too. Gradually other people started to drift in as well. And now the only people still clinging on in the real world where it rains and you get old and you get ill and you have to look at your ugly face in the mirror every day are people like me and my gradually dwindling band of customers."

"Are all these tanks full?"

"Mostly they were. But that's a good question."

"People die, I suppose."

"And normally babies are born to take their place."

Jason scratched his head. "Ah."

"Yes. If everyone's in the tanks living life virtually they're not out here bringing up kids. The schools closed down a long time ago in this town.

"There's no purpose for anyone anymore. Hell they even turned the Presidency over to an AI. Just distraction. Like the restaurant. I mean, nobody pays me for dinner because we no longer use money. I keep the place open because it gives me something to do and I like to see people. I guess they come because they're trying to pretend things are still normal. It can't be for the food. It's excellent, don't get me wrong. Only you can get better from any of the auto-cafe's because the expertise of every award-winning chef in history has been digitised and synthesised. We can't compete on quality. People only come because we're still human, warts and all."

"That won't last for ever."

"I know. I'm already looking for the next challenge. I've got some choices to make." Lucy bowed her head. "There has to be more. Or less." She let the thought hang.

"So you're going to go into one of those tanks?"

She laughed. "What? To become one of those Izos? That would be too sad, after all this time. We're among the last to hold out, you and me. What do you think will happen to the world if we joined the rest and went to live in fantasy land?" She smiled. "Ever been in the White House?"

The System Room lay in one of the basement layers of the V-corp building, deep in the heart of the city's business district. Unlike everywhere else he'd seen this building was well guarded with an array of automatic weapons systems and trip wires, plus a squad of oversized robot guards. But Lucy had the right ID biometrics and they passed unhindered.

They entered a large, empty room with banks of machinery lining the walls. She sat cross-legged on the floor and snapped her fingers. Suddenly they were in the Oval Office. Lucy, still cross-legged on the floor, gestured for Jason to take his place opposite her. Between them lay a dull silver briefcase. "Before you ask, we're here because this is where all the big decisions are taken."

"I was more interested in *how* we got here."

"This whole building's covered by a V field, attuned to my neural profile. It means we can access a virtual world here without using a tank or a band. If you ask me that's pretty dangerous technology – I'm just pleased we never had the chance to roll it out."

"What's that?" said Jason, pointing at the briefcase.

"The choice. Shall we?" Lucy put her hand on the briefcase's palm reader. The case sprang open, revealing ancient electronics and a bright red button. "Recognise this?"

"The nuclear trigger."

"It's not really a big red button, of course. But I've always wanted to press the big red button."

"What happens if you do?"

"The V-worlds are entirely run by AI super brains somewhere in a mountain in Wyoming. At least that's where we put them. I guess they could be anywhere by now thanks to the beauty of the cloud. Somewhere out of reach, anyhow."

"So?"

"So there's no off switch. No way to turn the worlds off. Except…"

"The red button is your back door, right?"

Lucy nodded. "One of the reasons I got canned is because I kept putting these fail-safes in the programmes. I thought by now the AI would have rooted them out and eliminated them, but I guess it likes to live a little dangerously. All I have to do is press this red button and every V-world on the planet switches off, simultaneously. Including that Refuge you think you came from."

He let the thought sink in and found he wasn't surprised. "So why haven't you done it?"

Lucy unfolded her legs, strolled over to a cupboard behind the presidential desk and brought out a bottle and two glasses. "Scotch. The finest." She poured and sipped appreciatively. "Did you see how miserable Drax was before he went back in the tank? And the anticipation on Hender and Butterfly's faces? I'm not sure I want their unhappiness on my consciousness, or that of the millions of other people sitting in those tanks living out their fantasies."

He tasted the whisky. He suspected it was as good as anything in the real Oval Office. "But in a couple of generations there'll be no humans left in the V worlds, just AI. And hardly anyone left out here. The big red button's the only way out."

"You see my dilemma."

"So you want me to make your decision for you."

"We could go into the tanks, live out our lives there. Most people don't even know they're in VR by now. It's easy to forget reality when it doesn't seem real."

He smiled. "Or to think something is real just because you want it to be. I know why you haven't pressed the red button now. You can't."

"And why might that be?"

"Because you're not real. None of this is. Not the Oval Office, not the warehouse. Only me."

She snorted. "Don't kid yourself. You haven't got the imagination to invent me."

"Really? This is my red button, isn't it? My way out."

He pressed the button.

Twins

Charlie passed the salt to Zack without being asked. He never needed to be asked, at least out loud.

"You're doing it now, aren't you?" said his mother, clearly not impressed.

"We're always doing it, Mama."

"Your father wishes you wouldn't."

Charlie glanced at his brother. "We don't actually have a choice."

"You always have a choice," said his mother.

"No we don't," the twins answered together, laughing.

"It's not funny," said their father, breaking his silence.

Charlie wished he could read his father's mind, the way he could read Zack's. But he didn't really need to gauge the emotions radiating from him like a furnace. Fear, suspicion, and betrayal.

He's mad 'cause we're leaving, he said to Zack. Mom looked over, puzzled, aware that they were talking telepathically. He knew his parents felt excluded by the link he had with Zack, by the closeness that it delivered that was far stronger than the parent child bond could ever be.

No, he's relieved. But he feels guilty, 'cause we're his boys and he knows he should love us.

And he's running out of opportunities to tell us what a disappointment we are.

Charlie wondered whether he should respond to his father with tact or rudeness, but then the food arrived and the moment passed.

Charlie and Zack ordered the same meal, of course. Chickpeas and spinach with more than a hint of chili. A glance over to his parents reminded Charlie how annoyed that made them, eating the same food, doing the same things. Mom ordered the, probably in some misguided attempt to get closer to them. Everybody knew she hated chickpeas.

His father, Davis Macall, nearly cancelled when he realised that the restaurant was called Veganomics. Steak was more his thing: blood red and dripping. The old man sat rigidly, like the proud man he was, holding his cutlery with surgical precision. His hair was short and grey now and gravity had pulled his thin, pinched face downwards. Charlie wondered if that was how he and Zack would look in a few years. No, they took after their mother too much. Heavier, stockier, shorter, with fuller, more rounded features. Nadine MacCall had been a beauty when she'd been younger, and her sons had inherited her easy, casual attractiveness.

Zack filled their mother in on all the mission details. "I'm the lucky one," he said. "I get to go to the stars."

Charlie wasn't so sure, and he hadn't argued much when Zack had run, anguished, to Mission Control when they'd first suggested Charlie should be the one to go. Zack got his way, of course, like he always did.

"Lucky?" she said. "I'll never see you again!"

Zack sighed. "They need me, Mom."

"Nonsense. They've got two other sets of twins. They don't need all three of you."

"Yes they do, Mom, Because…" Zack's sentence tailed off as Nadine picked up on the implications.

"Because they don't think you'll all make it."

"They're just being cautious, is all," said Charlie, putting his hand on his mother's arm. "They estimate the chances of failure are less than twenty percent, and that makes it almost certain we *will* make it."

"We're not a gambling family, Charles, never have been."

She'd clearly never seen them play cards, Zack at the table, getting all the attention, Charlie opposite, standing unobtrusively behind his opponents.

"They have to put us in cryo though. Otherwise we wouldn't be the same age at the other end. And they don't think the link will work so well if we've aged at different rates." Not to mention the fact that Charlie would be eighty four years old by the time the thirty three year old Zack arrived on Sanctuary, courtesy of speed of light time dilation. Seven years for Zack but fifty four for Charlie.

When the first set of twins had displayed proper telepathic powers, they'd been regarded as freaks and curios. But inevitably the scientists wanted to poke and prod until the limits of their abilities became apparent. They split the twin sons of an Idaho farmer up and sent one to Mars, and that's how they discovered that the communication between them was *instantaneous*. They shared thoughts with no gap at all, faster than the speed of light. And that made them a very precious commodity indeed.

"Well I don't know why anyone has to go at all." Nadine said, reaching for another glass of wine. Zack had said she was drinking more, but Charlie hadn't noticed until now.

"Because it's out there, Mom, said Charlie. "And because there are seventeen billion people on the planet and real estate is at a premium right now." Not to mention the upcoming war, the continued destruction of the ecosystem and the need to do something dramatic this side of the election.

"But our lives are *good* here," Nadine said. "We have money, a fine house…"

"And we get to eat in fancy restaurants like this one while half the population outside is starving to death." said Charlie. "And things are only going to get worse."

"Besides," added Zack, "It's just like Earth. Better, it's just like Earth used to be, before we started with all the pollution and the overpopulation. It's paradise, Mom."

We're getting out of here.

Charlie wasn't about to argue, with his mother on the verge of tears and his father staring ahead in silence.

"We'll be gone in the morning."

Their father nodded. Nadine took another drink. Zack and Charlie stood together, scraping their chairs back with such a unity of sound that other diners turned and stared. Nadine stood too, embracing first Zack then Charlie, sobbing.

Davis MacCall didn't stand, but he did nod once. Charlie started to put out his hand, but Zack pulled him back.

As they walked out into the cool rain Charlie risked a look back, but his parents had already left their table and, he realised, gone out of his life for ever.

Charlie and Zack discussed what they'd come to call the Last Supper as they ignored the briefing before the cryofreeze. They were in a military hospital with stark white walls and nurses in severe uniforms. The *New Beginning* launched in three days, and the twins needed to be deep frozen well before then. Charlie would be moved underground, to a secret location deep in the Rockies. Zack would be off into space.

Should we go back? Mom looked so sad, Charlie said.

She'll get over it. Zack held out his arm so one of the medical staff could inject the drug cocktail which would prepare the body for cryo.

There was nobody left to say goodbye to. No girlfriends, no wives. When your brother is constantly in your head it's difficult to have a relationship with anyone else, let alone girls, and it was maybe inevitable that they were leaving nobody behind.

Charlie settled back into the upholstered coffin that would be his home for fifty-four years. He began to feel drowsy.

Zack?

Uhuh?

You still there?

There was no reply. For the first time he could remember, Zack was no longer in his head.

Charlie woke, groggy, and waited for the seal to click open on his coffin. It released its gas with a sibilant hiss and slowly sprung open. He checked his chin for stubble, slightly disappointed that fifty-four years growth probably didn't even warrant a shave. He sat up and looked around. He'd seen images of this room in the pre-freeze briefing, but what he'd seen had been a brightly lit chamber filled with people and machinery. As he looked over the darkened, deserted cavern he wondered if he was in the same place. There should have been doctors. Something wrong then.

Zack? The silence he got in response told him something else was wrong, too.

He wondered where the others were. He'd barely noticed them at the briefing, because they weren't important then, and because he'd been arguing about something with Zack. But now, with his head silent, he had a strong desire for company.

He eased himself out of the coffin and dropped his bare feet onto the ground, settling not on the cool tiles he expected but on a thick layer of dust.

There were three coffins in the room, laid out side by side. Two coffins in was supposed to be Dee Nordstadt, whose twin Freya should currently be in orbit around Sanctuary. Assuming she'd made it. Twenty percent failure odds meant that statistically one of them wasn't likely to, and Charlie had always thought those odds had been doctored to reassure them.

Rolf Gaarder, a forty-five year old Norwegian, was supposed to be in the remaining chamber. As Charlie peered down at Rolf's partially desiccated corpse, he began to get a very uneasy feeling. Rolf had played the odds and lost.

Dee Nordstadt's chamber was empty, and that probably meant she was alive. Charlie sank to the ground. Very shortly he was unconscious.

When he woke the lights were on and someone was looking down at him.

"Had me worried there for a second," said Dee. She had short cropped spiky blonde hair which emphasised her Scandinavian heritage. "You okay?"

He lifted himself up on his elbows. "I'll live." He looked around. "Unfortunately."

She hauled him up. "Gotta be positive. Life is good."

"I can't hear Zack."

"I said life's good, not perfect. I can't hear Freya either."

"That means they're dead though, doesn't it?"

Charlie could see by her expression that he'd used up his quota of negative questions.

"No, it just means they're not awake yet."

He chanced one more. "But we were all supposed to wake at the same time."

"Hey, I've been awake for three days now, down here, alone, going slowly mad. Rolf's clock here says he'll be up sometime next Tuesday, not that it will do him any good, being dead and all. So much for our precision accurate clocks."

"Alone?"

She leaned back against her coffin. "Yeah, Completely. There's been no one down here for a long, long time."

"But the power?"

"Same geothermal source that's been powering the coffin batteries. But I don't entirely trust it, so I suggest we keep things dark as much as possible."

"But we're not staying here."

"Ah. And that's another problem." Dee dragged him to the elevator shaft and showed him the shredded wiring. "Looks like someone sliced the top end right off."

"Helpful. Staircase?"

"We're a third of a mile down. Still, in the interest of getting the hell out of here, I had a look." She opened a set of double doors next to the lift shaft. The insides were completely clogged with rocks. "So we're trapped."

"We're dead, then."

"Boy, you are a pessimist. This place was built to house a medical team of fifty. They may not be here, but their food certainly is."

"But we'll run out eventually."

"Not in our lifetimes."

Which are likely to be short and pointless, thought Charlie, but he didn't have time to say so because Dee had already disappeared round a turn in the corridor.

"C'mon," he heard her say, faintly, from what seemed far ahead. "All that talk of food is making me hungry."

The kitchen was large and well equipped. Dee set plates up on the central island while Charlie stood and watched, bemused. A lasagne steamed on the counter.

"I'm going to be charitable and assume you're too groggy to have noticed that I've done all the work here and you've just stood around. Just so long as you know that's the last time. One free pass, buddy. And pass the wine."

"Wine?"

"Sure, bottle's on the work surface. Should have aged nicely after all these years."

She took a tentative sip.

"Good?"

"Vinegar. Let's try another."

The second bottle was drinkable. Not good, exactly, but for the first time since waking Charlie started to relax.

"What do we do now?" said Charlie, once he'd started on his third glass.

"I have absolutely no idea," said Dee as she put her hand to her mouth to stifle a burp.

"There must me another way out."

"Tomorrow," she said, and reached for another bottle.

#

She knocked on his door with strong black coffee and a couple of pills. "Take 'em. If your hangover is half as bad as mine, you'll need them."

"I don't remember getting here." He looked back into the cramped cabin.

"You passed out. Again. Do that a lot?"

"Never."

"Well it has been fifty-four years since you had a drink."

"You too."

"I found the bottles three days ago. So I've had practice."

"I still can't hear Zack."

"Give it time."

"I think I'm going to throw up."

Later, they looked for another exit. The extent of their world was a series of rooms and interlinked corridors all circling the large chamber where they'd been held in stasis. There were maybe thirty rooms in total, ranging from meeting rooms to dormitories. There was even a weapons room, though there were no weapons in it. But there wasn't another exit.

"Agnes will know what to do," said Dee, later, over coffee.

"Agnes?"

"Rolf's sister. Didn't you pay any attention during the briefing? You and that idiot brother of yours just seemed to stare at each other with a glazed expression on your faces, like you were in lurve."

"Why don't you just say what you think? I mean, it's not as if anybody in here has feelings that you might hurt."

She grinned, not looking at all contrite. Charlie tried to feel offended but ended up grinning back.

"Sorry, kid," she said. "Truth is I'm a little scared and humour keeps me grounded. I didn't mean to cause offence."

"S'okay. I guess I wasn't really paying attention. But don't call me kid, okay? I may not remember that much of the briefing but I do remember you're only twenty eight."

"That's still three years older than you are, kid, so suck it up. Anyhow, back to Agnes."

"Did you know her from before?" he asked.

"What, you think because we're all Scandinavian that we all live in the same little village, surrounded by reindeer and wolves?"

"No wolves. Extinct."

"Look, you add Norway, Finland, Sweden and Denmark together and you have a hundred and fifty million people. Probably twice as many by now. So no, I didn't know Agnes from before."

"But you're related, right? That's why so many telepath twins are from Scandinavia."

"Kid, you and me are probably related. Where did you say your folks were from, originally?"

Oslo, he thought but didn't say. "Detroit."

"There you are," she sat back, looking smug. "You even lie like a Norwegian."

After dinner that second day they played chess. At first Charlie found it much harder without Zack to tell him where to move, but as the game progressed he found himself enjoying it more than he'd ever enjoyed any game of chess before. He still lost though, those first few times. He didn't win until the fifth game, and by then he had a suspicion she'd let him.

They relaxed after the game with a glass of wine, which was a habit he knew he couldn't afford to get used to. They'd had to try three bottles before they found an acceptable one and Charlie suspected their stocks might not last much longer.

"Fortunately, there's a lot of whisky back there. And that only gets better with age," she said, as if reading his thoughts.

"You weren't?"

She laughed. "No. Sometimes you don't have to read thoughts to know what someone's thinking."

"What am I thinking now?"

"Well," she put her finger on her chin and looked up at the ceiling. "You're wondering why this is so easy, all this talking to another person who isn't your brother."

He paused, unsure. "I was actually trying to work out what's going on."

"Weird stuff, probably. Beyond that I have no ideas."

"That doesn't sound like you."

"You saying I'm opinionated." She punched him lightly on the arm. "Well, since you insist, I think we've just been forgotten."

"Doesn't seem very likely. I mean, we were important back then."

"Back then is ancient history. And this place is expensive to run. Just the kind of long term project that Governments cut when they need to balance the books."

Charlie yawned. "Time for bed."

"Charlie?"

"Okay," he said in answer to her unasked question. "But only because I'm lonely too."

"Clothes on, okay? This is just about not having to wake up in the night and find the room's empty. So that when I ask a question, there's someone else there to answer it."

"Definitely."

"Even if you are a complete dork and nothing like as cool as Freya."

"And even though you're bound to steal the duvet and are nothing like as funny as Zack."

"Needs must."

"Exactly."

Charlie wasn't entirely sure at what point they dropped the clothes-on rule, but he woke up with a smile on his face and didn't realise he hadn't thought of Zack at all, until Dee sat up sharply and, as predicted, took the duvet with her.

"She's awake."

Charlie rubbed his eyes and sat up. "That's good, isn't it," he said, then realised that it wasn't. "I still can't hear Zack."

"She's confused, Disoriented. There's an alarm going off."

It works, then. Charlie hadn't quite believed they could pass messages between star systems. Mars was, well, just Mars. But Sanctuary was a long, long way away. "Zack?"

"Agnes is awake too."

"Zack?"

She turned, frowning. "They're looking at his coffin now. He's not moving."

"Zack!" A sudden stabbing pain sliced through Charlie's head. He let out a wail, then stopped, relieved. He'd know, wouldn't he? "He's not dead."

"No. But he's not moving. Agnes has gone to get some medical equipment."

"Where are they?"

"In orbit, apparently. I don't know why they haven't landed. There are other people waking now."

The crew. Charlie had forgotten. There would be a doctor. In the end Agnes poured cold water on Zack's face and he woke up, spluttering.

"Ow" Charlie said, holding his head.

"Awake then."

"And screaming."

"That's good, isn't it?"

Hey.

Hey.

You okay?

Did it work?

You tell me. You're the one orbiting a new planet.

Orbiting?

Talk to me when you've caught up.

159

Charlie glanced over and saw Dee frowning.

"That staring into space thing, Is that what we do?"

"Uhuh. Didn't you realise?"

Dee stayed mostly quiet for the next hour or so, staring at the wall no doubt locked in conversation with her sister. With Zack and Freya awake again something had changed, and Charlie wasn't sure how he felt about that.

Not at all what we'd been promised, Charlie boy. Looks like you got the best of the deal after all.

Why are you still in orbit?

Because most of the planet's radioactive, as far as the sensors can tell. Nowhere safe for us to land.

What? The sensors…

That was fifty four years ago. More, because the data had to come back at the boring old speed of light. A lot's happened since then, believe me.

It's been bombed?

Looks like it.

Charlie shook his head and looked over at Dee, clearly having a similar conversation to the one he was having with Zack.

Charlie?

Later.

"You getting the same information as me?"

Dee snapped back into the room. "Sounds grim."

Who are you talking to?

A pause. Why didn't he want to tell him? He struggled to contain his thoughts, but he could never keep anything from Zack. His raw, unfiltered response leaked.

Shut up. Too late to take it back.

Zack's responded with a stab of rage. *No I won't shut up.* Charlie could feel Zack trying to control his anger. *She looks just like Freya, so I can understand. Just stay focused.*

I am focused. Just not on you. He wasn't sure if he'd transmitted that last thought.

"Distracted?"

"Hard to have two conversations at once."

"Switch him off then."

"What do you mean, switch him off?"

"You know, leave the phone off the hook?"

He didn't realise he could do that, But that was going to have to be a discussion for later. Right now he needed to make sense of what was going on.

Agnes worried them. In the madness of the first few hours Zack and Freya barely noticed her, and it was one of the crew who found her slumped against a bulkhead, staring into space. Thy led her to a cabin, laid her on the bed and left her there, motionless, having refused all attempts by the crew to communicate.

They knew more now, though, about the predicament they were in, because the ship had been getting light speed feeds from Earth. The only trouble was, neither Zack nor Freya would tell them what the news was. Not until they got to the surface. Typical Zack, he thought. Always in his head. Always keeping secrets.

Charlie and Dee shared a cabin again that night, even though their siblings had woken.

"What you said, before? About switching him off."

So she showed him.

The ship had a comprehensive database holding most of the library stock of the planet, including the military stuff. Including base schematics. Including a way for Charlie and Dee to get out. There was a backdoor, apparently, in the pantry, behind all those stacks of dried food.

I couldn't feel you. What did you do? Zack sounded annoyed.

Must be the distance. Everything's unpredictable.

Not everything. You're still annoying.

Charlie switched him off again.

It took them an hour to find the door, and another hour to clear all the pallets of food away from it. There were supposed to be robots down there to do that kind of heavy lifting but the only one they'd found was missing an arm

161

and a power pack, clearly cannibalised for spares. Whatever forced the medical team to the surface had, it seemed, included the robots.

Eventually they found another staircase, this time completely free of fallen rocks. The lights didn't seem to work so they used head torches. Charlie looked straight up but he couldn't see the top.

"A third of a mile. We should take sandwiches."

Charlie took the pack Dee offered him – not just sandwiches, judging by the weight, and led the way up the stairs.

It took them an hour and a half, including a lengthy rest half way up when the staircase opened up into a room sized chamber with chairs, tables and a couple of vending machines filled with ancient chocolate and soft drinks. Charlie was exhausted by the time the stairs levelled off and opened up into a long, wide passage. The heavy bulkhead door at the end was locked.

"Any ideas?" Dee punched the door, which gave off a dull metallic thud.

"Nope." Charlie looked around, but the corridor was empty. "Nothing here we can use either."

A control panel on the corridor wall to the left of the door had a numeric keypad and a display panel. The panel was dead. "No power," said Dee. "I bet when the power went up here the deadlocks engaged automatically."

"Sounds plausible. What do we do?"

"Turn the power back on of course." She pulled the backpack off Charlie and started poking around in it, before pulling out a large battery pack.

"What, you *anticipated* this?"

"Didn't you?"

It took ten minutes, but Dee managed to get the power back on. The panel glowed, but the door remained bolted. Charlie's chest tightened. He felt his resolve disappearing. He needed to re-establish the link with Zack, to absorb his brother's calm confidence, even though that would give

Zack power over him again. But then he looked over at Dee, looking purposefully at the panel, as if trying to work out a puzzle, not fall apart in a crisis. "Conclusions?" said Dee.

"We can't do this by ourselves. There's a passcode, and we don't have it."

"Agreed."

"The twins have access to the base schematics."

Reluctantly, Charlie opened the link.

I know what you're doing. Freya told me.

No time for that.

Annoyed though Zack clearly was, he pulled up the door codes. Charlie pressed the sequence and heard the deadbolts snap back. He took a deep breath and looked at Dee. "Shall we?"

They stepped through together.

"Oh my," he said, as he looked out over the ruined wasteland that was once Wyoming.

"What happened to the mountains?"

Not a living thing was visible. The ground was covered in grey ash, whipped by a wind which took his breath away. Overhead the sky had an unnatural murky blackness.

Dee tugged at his backpack again. "Hold still. Looking for the Geiger counter." She tugged hard and produced a dull metal box. She switched it on and they looked down at its crystalline display.

"Amber, surprisingly," she said. "That means we're not about to cook. Whatever happened here happened a while ago. It's still radioactive, but so long as we don't spend too much time out here, we should be okay."

"Back inside?"

"Oh yes."

Charlie realised his brother could have killed him by not warning him about the radiation. Once safely inside, he restored the link. They talked as he and Dee descended the long staircase back to the base.

I know you're mad, but…

Why didn't you warn me?

Charlie thought Zack had broken the link for a moment, but eventually his brother replied. *Wanted to, bro', but truth is, we had no idea what to warn you about. All we know is that Earth's gone very quiet. I know you're pretty dumb but Freya thought Dee would be sensible enough to take precautions. You're wearing radiation suits, right?*

Why would be wearing radiation suits?

But you are all right, right?

That's not the point.

They sparred for a while until Charlie's annoyance turned into exasperation and he realised he had nothing left to say. Soon he was back at the room with the vending machines. Dee sat down heavily on one of the hard plastic seats and Charlie followed her lead. Charlie had found out nothing useful from Zack but Dee seemed to have been having a more adult conversation. She filled him in.

"Apparently there was a war, about five years after we were frozen. That's probably when this base was shut down. No hint that it was nuclear, though. Before we lost contact we knew that the other side was winning."

"Who?"

"The African Alliance, not that it matters much. We think our side managed to keep the colony programme secret. Whether that's true or not mission control certainly stopped beaming messages out into space. That was forty-two years ago."

"Looks like something happened after that."

She sat up straight and smiled. "Got an idea, Grab your backpack."

She smiled even more broadly when the plan actually worked. As soon as they got back to the base Dee powered up the computer array. Freya provided the codes, and she was in.

Earth, from space, filled a giant screen which descended from the roof. "Earth may be a radioactive pile of rubble but it doesn't mean the satellites aren't still working."

Charlie was surprised. Surely a nuclear war would fry any communications arrays.

"This feed's from a high one. About as far out as you can get and still be in orbit. Military. Designed to be out of range of any inconvenient electromagnetic pulses," said Dee, as if anticipating his thoughts. "Hmm." She peered forwards and looked at the data pouring out. "Unless they developed some pretty strange weapons since we left, this mess doesn't look man made. I'm no expert but it seems to me that this much damage should be glowing right now. It's radioactive, sure, but not nearly enough."

Thick grey cloud covered the planet. They had to imagine what lay beneath.

Gotta tell you. Zack. Looks pretty grim down there.

Here too. Some energy readings we haven't seen before.

Swap data?

Whatever had happened to Earth had happened to Sanctuary too. Same strange readings, same devastation.

"I think we need to start on the whisky," he said, turning to Dee.

"You read my mind."

There was something in orbit around Sanctuary, and it didn't look man made. The *New Beginning* hauled it in.

Definitely alien. Some sort of weapon.

Do you think you should have it on board then?

It's dead now. Bet if you look closely I bet you'll see something similar in orbit around Earth.

But why?

Ah, a question for the philosophers. Personally, I don't care, so long as whoever set it doesn't come back.

Charlie and Dee developed a scotch-fuelled theory that it was the war that triggered some sort of over the top reaction with whatever aliens destroyed both planets. Maybe they were spooked at thought of a nasty aggressive species with nuclear weapons which seemed quite prepared to use them. Or maybe they took one look at humanity and decided that the universe could live without it. Whatever the reason, Charlie doubted they'd be back to mop up the survivors.

It didn't feel much like survival. There were only two of them, and they were trapped, deep underground. But he didn't feel like giving up, and he wondered why. It wasn't just Dee, though she was certainly an interesting new development in his life. Then came news from the *New Beginning*, and he finally understood.

Agnes never left her cabin. On the third day they found her in a pool of her own blood, eyes open, gazing into nothingness. She left a one word note. "Alone."

"Much as I like you, Charlie, if it's just you and me it's going to feel pretty lonely down here too."

"But it's not just us, is it?"

She nodded, "Even though they irritate the hell out of us, knowing Freya and Zack are out there going through the same stuff makes it important that we hold it all together."

"Knowing that there's something other than this."

"Exactly. We keep going for them as much as they do for us."

The colonists want to come home.

Charlie sighed, rolled over and pulled away, dragging the bed sheet with him and leaving Dee's nakedness exposed.

"Zack?"

"Uhu."

"Picks his moments. Tell him you're busy."

What do you mean? he asked Zack instead.

Dee frowned, punched Charlie gently on the shoulder and eased herself out of bed. "Or I could make coffee."

What I said. This planet has turned into Earth's evil twin. If we stay here it'll be under extruded domes until we're all old and grey, and that's without mentioning the heavy gravity, barely breathable atmosphere and unpleasant alien rodents. About all that survived, apart from the bugs. No one wants that. Whereas you have a nice comfortable mountain.

It's not paradise.

Best on offer.

Dee returned with the coffee.

"The colony's coming home. Zack doesn't want to."

I didn't say that!

Charlie ignored him. If Zack had been happy he's have said *he* wanted to come home, not the colonists. "It'll take years. They'll be in stasis, but…"

"…they'll be out of contact." She went quiet, talking, Charlie presumed, to Freya. "They want us to go back in stasis too. Wake up when they get here."

Charlie frowned. Could the ageing equipment handle it? What about the failure rate?

"We could die," said Dee echoing his thoughts, though clearly talking to Freya.

Do it, you selfish bastard, shouted Zack.

So they set the equipment up, prepared themselves as best they could and waited for the signal from Zack and Freya that meant they were on ship and about to enter stasis themselves.

Charlie waited until Zack was asleep to talk. Zack got angry whenever Charlie switched him off, so it became easier to find other ways to talk privately with Dee.

"We are doing the right thing."

"Convincing yourself or me?" said Dee.

"With this equipment I'm not sure both of us will make it."

"If we don't do it, then we'll probably never hear from Freya and Zack again. Can you live with that?"

"We'll be alone here."

"No, Charlie, we won't. Apart from the obvious fact that we've got each other, do you really believe we're the sole survivors of whatever happened here? I'm betting this isn't the only subterranean bunker."

"That's not what I meant and you know it. When you've had someone else in your head constantly for the whole of your life it's difficult to visualise anything different. It's almost as if we're the same person sometimes, just in different bodies."

"Trapped for eternity. In my case with a needy sister who's beginning to irritate the hell out of me, and in your case with a guy who always wants the final say. No, Charlie, we won't be alone. And, more importantly, we'll be free."

With Zack in his head Charlie had never really had to make a choice before. And that, ultimately, was what persuaded him.

Freya had a complete meltdown when Dee told her they weren't going under. Zack's response was more subtle. He behaved as he always had when Charlie tried to exert his will: he ignored him, knowing that Charlie would give in eventually.

Except this time he didn't.

Charlie and Dee closed down the stasis tanks and set to work finding other survivors.

As he went under, Zack screamed.

One night Dee emerged from the kitchen with an almost empty bottle and a frown.

"Last one." She poured into two small glasses, eking out the dregs.

He swirled his glass, took a sip and eased back in his seat, enjoying the warmth of the single malt. "I don't think of Zack much anymore."

"Freya too. I don't think she ever forgave me for hooking up with you."

"They would never have let us if they'd been awake."

"For the first time I was able to make my own mind up without having to consider her." She grinned. "You're happier without him, aren't you?"

Charlie's answer was measured. "And that makes me very sad." He paused, took a sip. "I always used to think Zack was my crutch. My excuse for never having to interact properly with anyone else. But my mother was right. We do have a choice."

He drained his glass and savoured the last mouthful. Harsher than he remembered. He realised he wouldn't miss it much after all.

Hunter

Kyle Hunter had been miserable ever since they'd left Earth orbit. Maybe because of the body count: three so far and probably more to come. Or maybe the moral ambiguity. He hated moral ambiguity.

He cracked his knuckles and stared at the wall. Follow the chain, secure the line. Easy. Except someone else was following the chain too, and link by link it was breaking. He'd had a feeling this one was going to go wrong.

He'd been hired by a rich guy whose son was dying, only kept alive by a rare and valuable drug which shouldn't exist at all. Then the supplier turned up with a hole in his head. And when the dealer next up in the chain ended up face down in the river the rich guy panicked and called in Kyle.

The chain led to a lowlife called Bill Higgs, and a leisure cruiser on the slow route to Solaria. He spent ten long and uneventful days watching Higgs eat, get drunk and try and pick up women. On the eleventh he started getting twitchy. Kyle sat at a table in a dark corner of a bar. Higgs stood at the counter, taking a call. Odd, because nobody could call from outside the ship and he was travelling alone.

Then Higgs ran out into the corridor. Kyle jumped out of his seat right into the back of a large man in a tasteless green jacket, spilling his drink. By the time he'd avoided the fist that came his way, Higgs was gone. He cursed at his stupidity. His instincts were off, probably because he was bored. Always stand between the mark and the door. Always.

Ten minutes later Higgs floated past the aft portholes. He wasn't wearing a space suit.

That was two days ago, which left Kyle plenty of time to wonder why a routine seek and find assignment threw up so many dead people.

The ship's background hum shifted slightly. They were about to dock.

The security line trailed down a hundred metres of corridor and almost back into the ship. Kyle found himself deep in conversation with a small round woman with an animated face and a beaming smile. In truth, he had things to think about and plans to make, but the woman wanted to talk and Kyle was happy to let her.

"ID," said the border guard, looking past Kyle's left shoulder and frowning. Kyle smiled at him. He looked like he was having a bad day.

"I think my good friend Vera here was first. You have a nice day now, Vera. And don't forget to give those grandkids of yours a big hug." He winked for effect.

Vera's smile was infectious. By the time Kyle took his place at the head of the line the guard had softened enough for full eye contact.

"Such a nice lady, don't you think?" Kyle said, "Here to see her family. She had photos. So cuuute."

The guard barely looked at the ID as he passed it through the reader. "Welcome to Solaria," he said, already looking past Kyle to the next man in line. A light flicked from red to green and he stepped forward.

He waited for his luggage to catch up. The station was old, practically antique, and by the sound of the wheezing coming from the luggage platform's antigrav, full of junk way past its use by date. Kyle sniffed the air: stale, with the unmistakable harshness of a million recyclings. Failing filters too, well past their specified lifespans. He walked down the metal ramp in the centre of the crowded chamber and made the call.

"Boss," said Suarez, in his implant.

"Bar in thirty."

Suarez got there first. Kyle spotted her as soon as he walked in, at a bar stool, with some guy hitting on her. Kyle wasn't surprised: she got that sort of attention everywhere, despite the fact that she appeared hard enough to crack rocks just by looking at them. Maybe that was the appeal. Dyed red spiky hair, tight leather and Angels tattoos didn't do it for Kyle but he guessed some men would warm to the challenge. Some women, too. With Suarez on the team life was never dull.

Kyle sidled up to the bar and took his seat two stools down from the guy, with Suarez on the opposite side. He caught her eye and winked.

He was on his second drink when the guy finally left, alone. Suarez moved on up. "I'm supposed to meet him later, on his yacht. Can't wait." She rolled her eyes.

"Be nice."

"He wants to take me down to the planet to see the aliens. Apparently they're quite cute. Clever, too."

"Yeah, well, they're supposed to be off limits," said Kyle. "Not that that ever stops you."

"There might be a connection between the aliens and the guy we're looking for. Seems unlikely, but that's what I hear."

"You found him yet?"

Suarez gestured to the barman, who brought over a beer: bottled, some fancy South American import. Kyle was always astonished that sort of thing could travel so far and sell so cheap. "Not quite," Suarez took a deep swig, "But he's here."

"He's left traces?"

"No traces."

"Then how can you tell he's here? You psychic?"

"*Because* he left no traces," she continued, swigging her beer again. Two swigs, one empty bottle. She gestured for another.

"So where is he?"

Suarez looked sheepish. "Working on it."

"So we're going to have to do this the old fashioned way then."

"Excellent," said Suarez, draining her drink.

"Starting with checking the ships' manifest. Who's loaded what, and when."

"Not so excellent. That sounds dull."

They headed for the ship's office.

"Yes?" The girl didn't look up. They were in a large antechamber, furnished with expensive looking wooden furniture, fancy pictures and silk hangings in delicate shades of crimson and russet. Beyond the girl's overlarge desk were carved oak doors. She was partially hidden behind a potted plant, reading something on a hand-screen. Everything looked new, brightly lit and freshly painted, right down to the streak of red across the girl's lips and the bright white streaks in her jet-black hair.

"We'd like to see the Station Director," said Kyle. Suarez shifted impatiently from foot to foot next to him.

The girl leaned back in her seat, looked him up and down, glanced sideways at Suarez and then went back to her screen. She was young and hot and Kyle just knew she had more interest in chewing her gum than helping him out. "Not happening."

He sighed. Suarez tensed. He considered smiling but you needed eye contact for that and besides, she was young therefore he was invisible. Kyle held Suarez back gently with his hand. "I'm here on behalf of Station Control", he said. "The Director asked for our help."

She looked up. "Unlikely for two reasons," she said. "First, he never asks for help. He doesn't need it. And second I don't know about it. And I know everything." She looked down again.

"You're very sure of yourself, Miss…"

"You don't need to know my name. "

"Miss Paula Kendrie. At least that's what your name plate says."

She peered at her hand-screen. "And according to this you're Mr Carson Yeung. At least that's what the ID you

174

passed through security says. Trouble is, the bioscan I've just done on you says you're Kyle Hunter. Now what am I to believe?"

Kyle shrugged. "If you know who I am you know I need to see the Director."

She looked about to say something else but then Kyle heard a click and the great oak doors swung open. A small man in a dark blue suit poked his head out.

"I'll take it from here, Paula."

And they were in.

Ronan Prentiss was a short, stocky man in an expensive suit. Kyle guessed his bulk was flab, not muscle.

They sat on large blue sofas and exchanged small talk, as if on a social call. Kyle looked around. The room gave a real contrast to the rest of the station. It was big, for one thing, and serene, with gentle air-conditioning that stripped out the staleness pervading the rest of the station. The whole place smelled newly decorated, with fine pictures on the wall and opulent furniture artfully scattered in all the right places. He wondered how much it all cost.

His bionics alerted him to a large number of hidden cameras and recording devices. He would have been surprised if he hadn't found any. Still, their extent and sophistication alarmed him. A look at Suarez suggested she felt the same.

And then Prentiss was ready to talk business. "To what do we owe the pleasure of your visit, Mr Hunter?"

"You've probably guessed we're on a security mission." Kyle waved airily. "Just routine. We're checking out the movements to and from the station." He leaned forward. "We think there might be people passing through the station who really shouldn't be, if you know what I mean. Criminals, and illegals, looking for a new life on Minerva."

Prentiss sat back in mock shock. "Surely not, I mean, how would they get past our border patrols?"

"I did," said Kyle. "Or at least Carson Yeung did."

"Point taken," said Prentiss. "My office is at your disposal of course. What can I do to help?"

"Thank you, but we can handle it. This is a courtesy call. Naturally we'll let you know if we find anything."

They got up to leave. At the door Kyle turned. "Oh, one thing you could help us with. Cargo manifests for the last two weeks. Probably useless but we've got to be thorough, right?"

Paula Kendrie was filing her nails as they passed her desk. She didn't smile.

"What was that about?" said Suarez as they headed down the corridor.

"Switch to English," said Kyle. She nodded. "We can't assume this place isn't rigged for audio. Actually we can assume it is, judging by the level of the surveillance equipment in Prentiss's office. Seeing Prentiss means we're tagged now."

"That's unfortunate."

"Inevitable. Besides, we've got our target now."

"Yeah he does kind of flaunt it. Don't suppose we'll get the cargo manifests off him though."

Kyle shook his head. "Oh we'll get them all right. Suitably doctored of course. That should confirm things." He smiled. "I can't believe we've been so lucky. I mean, there I go, hoping to get some help from the Station Director to catch the bad guys and turns out he probably *is* the bad guys."

"Easy money, boss."

Kyle stopped walking. "One thing I've learned, Suarez. It's never easy."

Kyle needed to think, so he left Suarez to work though the manifests and headed for the observation deck. Because the station rotated it looked like the great crimson ball of Minerva was spinning around him, over his head and back round past his feet. That was unnerving, and probably explained why he was the only person on the deck. He got a coffee from the automated dispenser and sat on a bench facing the window.

Kyle wondered if he should be protecting Prentiss. After all, he needed him alive, if only so that he could follow him up the chain. He must be near the source now. To get so far only to fail would be frustrating.

The drug was medicinal, using a substance discovered twenty years ago. The team who presented it to the world wouldn't say what the source was, only that it was extremely rare. Everybody assumed it probably came from whatever was left of the Amazon rainforest, but the secretive team of scientists wasn't around anymore to confirm that because they'd all died in a plane crash.

The media called the drug Life, because that's what it provided. Unexpected plane crashes aside, Life seemed to stop whatever you were dying from in its tracks. A cell regenerating, anti-viral, age defying miracle.

And believed lost along with the scientists. Gradually people forgot about the drug that briefly promised the impossible. But some supplies were clearly getting through from somewhere. Why would anyone want to prevent that?

Suarez was hunched over a screen when Kyle got to the suite they'd rented for the mission. Actually 'suite' was a serious case of overselling. But it had beds, chairs, a desk for Suarez to do her stuff on and, something Kyle thought particularly important at this juncture, a mini-bar.

There's something in Bay Thirteen we should look at. A shipment, waiting for pickup," she said.

"From the contact?"

"The one who got spaced? The very same. I've got a time too. We need to be there in twenty minutes."

Kyle shook his head. "Haven't you noticed that there are security cameras covering every inch of the station? Wasn't it you who told me that in the first place? We'd never get anywhere close."

"Good job you've got a computer genius on the team who can hack the station's security systems and subvert all the camera feeds then."

"Can you really do that?"

"Done it. But I need to keep monitoring them. You'll have to do this one without me."

"Then I'm on my way."

The door to Bay Thirteen gave with a slight tug of equalising pressure, and a low hiss of onrushing air as atmosphere from the station drifted into the thinner mix in the bay. The cold was normal for a cargo hold, of course, but there was something else about this chill.

The lights took a few seconds to come up to full illumination and at first Kyle could only see piles of unopened storage crates neatly stacked against the far wall. Then as his eyes adjusted he noticed something else. A body, slumped against the crates.

Whoever it was had half his face missing. Kyle looked away.

And then the cargo bay got mighty crowded. Director Prentiss stood at the doorway in full silhouette, flanked by four security guards carrying very big guns. A set up, thought Kyle, just like he'd expected. One guard is precautionary, two is comprehensive, three is paranoia but four? Four is a tip-off.

Prentiss ambled forward, stopping inches from Kyle's face. "You're being arrested for the murder of whoever this is. But you know that, right?"

He turned to his men. "Take him away."

Kyle was led to a small grey featureless room with a plain table in the middle. On one side was a comfortable chair which Prentiss sat in. On the other was a stool which the guards pushed Kyle onto. He tried his implant and cursed when he got nothing but static. The guards left the room.

Kyle smiled. "Aren't you worried I'm going to lean across the table and take you out?"

Prentiss smiled back and leaned forward, prodding the air between them with his finger. It shimmered with the unmistakeable sheen of a force field. "No. You're going to kill yourself in a minute Mr Hunter. Nasty business. Not a lot I could do about it sitting over here. I guess I'm just going to have to watch you die. Could be painful, could be not. Depends."

"On?"

"How co-operative you are." He leaned back, as if contemplating which question he should ask. "Who are you working for?"

Kyle smiled. "You know I'm not going to tell you that."

Prentiss looked vacantly through him and Kyle guessed that he was activating something with his implant. The air in Kyle's part of the room started to get noticeably thinner. "Are you sure?"

Kyle shifted uncomfortably. "I'm freelance. Following a trail. To you."

"Me?"

"We both know what you're doing."

Prentiss laughed. "I have no idea what you're talking about." The air started to get thinner still. "You obviously want to die the painful way."

"I'm not keen on dying at all. Look. Why would I kill the guy in the cargo bay then stand over the body? And what did I kill him with? I wasn't carrying a gun or you would have found it on me."

"You stashed it somewhere, obviously."

"Did I? Don't you have video footage of me entering the room, without a gun? Come to that, don't you have footage of me *in* the room, finding him dead?"

"No. The cameras in the room malfunctioned. I need you to tell me how you managed that."

Kyle had difficulty breathing. "Half right, Prentiss," he gasped. "Someone is killing everyone in your distribution chain. But it's not me."

Kyle could hear sounds from outside the room. Prentiss turned, distracted. Something thudded to the floor. Then Kyle heard a gunshot, and another. And then the lights went out.

The door opened to a dark corridor with faint emergency strips giving off a low sullen glow. As Prentiss shifted in his chair, a small round figure walked in, picked up the gun lying on the table and looked at it as if not quite knowing which end to point.

And then she sliced a neat hole in the back of his head.

Vera. She glanced over at Kyle and smiled, nodded her head and walked out the way she'd come in, casually dropping the gun on the floor.

The lights went back on. And the force screen was down. "Suarez!" he called through his implant as he ran down the corridor. He almost tripped over one of the guards lying dead on the ground – Vera's work, he guessed. He felt the familiar static pulse. With Prentiss dead his implant was operational again.

"Boss!"

"Still alive. but I'm a bit busy. If you needed to get off this ship in a hurry, how would you do it?"

She hesitated before replying. "You bailing on me?"

"Never – but our killer is. Any ideas?"

"I'd head for the hangar they keep the private yachts in."

"Where?"

"Deck five. You're right on top of it."

Kyle dived into the nearest elevator. He was out of breath when he got to the hangar. The doors were partially open and Kyle could see a white pleasure yacht hovering outside. Vera stood in the middle of the vast open hangar space, looking up at the stars.

"Fascinating isn't it, the way that it looks as though we're completely exposed to space. And yet a little screen of force is keeping all that nasty hard vacuum out there and keeping us safe and warm in here."

"You're the killer."

"Yes. They deserved it, I guess. Though my employers didn't much care what happened to them as long as the shipments stopped."

Kyle nodded. "They won't stop, you know. Whoever is handling things down on the planet will set up another distribution chain."

"Yes but I'm following things back to their source, remember?"

The hangar doors were almost completely open now and the yacht began its slow glide through the force screen and onto the deck. It large, sleek and white, modelled after the old sailing ships it was named after.

"Do you know what they extract the drug from, Hunter?"

Kyle shook his head. "Plant. Rock. Dunno."

"From the spinal cords of the intelligent life form down there. It's a painful process. They keep them alive and in agony for days until they're eventually sucked dry. Then they let them die and they go and find another victim."

Kyle was still absorbing that when his implant pinged.

"Movement, boss. From the other hangar."

"I thought you had it all shut down?"

"This is on a separate circuit. Put in for the Director. Just in case."

"But he's dead."

Vera winked as she boarded her yacht. Kyle looked on, thought about small trusting aliens dying in agony and decided to let her go.

#

In Prentiss' escape flyer Paula Kendrie settled back and let calm soothing music wash over her. A setback, to be sure. But there were other ways to get shipments off planet. Working close to Prentiss so she could get his executive system access codes had been useful but let's face it, Prentiss was an ass and the station was boring. She missed being close to the action. She enjoyed seeing the look of incomprehension on those little alien faces as her guys held them down so she could plunge the needle into their weedy little backs.

And because she was drifting off to sleep she didn't notice Vera's yacht creep up slowly behind her…

Click

Santana pulled clear abruptly, tendrils of electric flame sweeping from her finger ends.

"Yah!"

Johnjon smiled. "Gotcha."

"Battle's not the war. Just you remember that."

"Jack back second try?"

So they both slid back into the game loop, letting the neural contacts work their magic. The game required fingertip contact to stay on line. Break the contact, lose the game. Since this was a PainGame, this was a test of stamina as much as a battle of wits, and Johnjon had stamina in abundance.

The room melted into a bright green field, replete with daisies and cowpats. Santana cursed. It was JJ's call on battleground since he'd won the first face-off. He knew she hated nature. Wildlife made her nervous, especially the idyllic sort. There'd be a lake over the next hillock, for sure. With swans and sailing boats.

She crouched on her knees and looked around, checking for danger points. JJ was out of sight, which was no surprise. He wasn't the sort for a quick kill. Make her suffer first. She tried to remember the parameters of this program block: found she couldn't. Snakes? Undoubtedly. Paradise is the deadliest place around.

She could hear his breathing. Right behind her.

She turned fast, getting to her feet and kicking out in one practised manoeuvre. Kicking fresh air.

"Damn." Santana ran for cover. A wooded copse a hundred metres left of her. The bastard was playing with her. If he'd had his weapon operative she'd have been finished. Well he was going to regret that.

Panting, she collapsed behind the first available tree. She patted the bulge on her left leg. Good. Neuro-pistol. Five shot charge. She figured JJ would have opted for the pulse rifle. Rules say that's a two shot weapon. Santana brought her pistol out and inspected it. It would probably take two clear shots to take JJ down, maybe more. She doubted if she could withstand even one rifle hit. And that was if the snakes didn't get her first. This game was real, frighteningly real. Santana winced. There must be easier ways of settling your differences.

Mars One. When the bubble burst MarsCo was screwed and investors scurried back into Earth stocks. That meant Marsbase cutbacks. Santana was damned if she was going to be on the return ticket list. Trouble was, so was JJ. Ex-lovers make the biggest double crossers and Santana couldn't believe he'd challenged her for the last remaining place on the base. MarsCrew wanted the best, able to survive anything fate could toss at them, hence Killzone.

Rules were simple. Crash twice out of different habitats and you lose the game. Your sanity, too, if you're not careful. First test, neutral ground. Then the winner chooses the second stage. Gets first choice on weapons too. Rifle, neuro-pistol, knives, flight pack, grenades, lucky dip. All with different handicaps. Fighting dirty definitely allowed.

Which suited Santana just fine.

At the edge of her hearing she felt she could detect a gentle sound. The wind? She'd almost forgotten what that sounded like. No. Someone moving. Not someone, something. Stalking her. Silently, she got to her feet, resting against the tree trunk. The sound came from further in the woodland. She gripped the pistol tight.

She edged forward, crackling wind dry grass as she went. A flash of brown in front of her. Then another. Then a third. Great. Three of them. Desperately she looked for cover. No point in returning to the clearing. JJ'd pick her off in an instant. But whatever was in front of her did not sound friendly. Stand and fight then.

Standoff. Minutes passed. Santana relaxed. She was imagining things. Then a rush and something brown and snarling was at her throat. Santana cried out, dropped

184

heavily, brought her arms together tight. The thing span back for a second, letting Santana get a good look. Quadruped, mainly fur and teeth, dripping rabidly. It sprang for another attack, but this time Santana was too quick for it. Her pistol seemed to grow out of her hand then - pump - the creature dropped in front of her.

Four shots left. This habitat was going to wipe her pistol clean before she came anywhere near JJ. And furball's two friends were lurking.

She backed into the tree, then knew instinctively what she had to do. Seconds later she was five metres high, looking down on two snarling animals noisily trying to bite her legs off. They couldn't get her. But she couldn't get down either. And their noise was going to tell JJ exactly where to find her.

That would probably have been it if JJ hadn't been such a cocky bastard.

He came in with a flame-thrower. Where the hell he got one of those was completely beyond Santana at first. Then she remembered that these scenarios had built in secrets.

The two furballs got flambéed. Then JJ looked up at Santana. He hoisted the flame-thrower on his left shoulder and prepared to fire.

Mistake. The weight of the flame-thrower, virtual or not, hampered his movements. And Santana was gravity assisted. The instant she saw him beneath her she dropped, both legs kicking. First leg took out the flame-thrower, second kick took out the swagger. Then she was off through the trees, scarcely able to believe her luck that JJ had eliminated the furballs for her.

But the game wasn't over yet. Far from it. JJ was winded, not down. And he still had the rifle. The odds were against her, she knew, but they'd been against her when she started this challenge and they'd probably still be against her if she won. JJ was a fighting expert on two levels: in mundane real life he'd been in the military, and in virtual life he was regular podium chief in whatever

185

game competition was going. Santana, on the other hand only jacked in at Christmas and Labor Day, and then only to get her ass whipped by her young nephews.

She had to think. What would JJ expect her to do? Stand in the clearing and wait to be gunned down, that's what. What wouldn't he expect?

JJ caught up with her five minutes later standing, doe like, in the centre of the clearing. He smiled, cocked his rifle. Fired.

Santana dropped like a stone. JJ's smile broadened. Then he realised they were still jacked in. Puzzled, he crept forward. He doubted whether Santana could stand the pain from a full rifle bolt and stay connected, but it was possible. He needed to check the kill.

Santana heard his footfall crunch the grass. JJ had just made his second mistake. He moved the rifle to loose the second killer pulse, but it was too late. He'd come in too close, as she knew he would. And that meant he was close enough to fall for an old trick.

She kicked out, swinging round to cuff the back of his legs by the knees. Surprised, he dropped. Then, pistol to forehead, she shot quickly, sharply.

They were thrown back out of the game.

"Gotcha."

JJ didn't smile.

The rules said they got a break at this stage, and Santana for one certainly needed one. JJ slunk off without a glance in her direction after they'd jacked out. Apart from the massive headache he must have, the humiliation of being suckered in such a way must have been galling. And the shame of going down to a single neuro-pistol shot - surely a first, but then nobody probably gets that close - must have been hard to take. Santana would have been willing to bet JJ was kicking himself for allowing a Base-wide observer link into the action.

She felt her shoulder, still aching from the memory of JJ's rifle impact. She'd guessed that JJ wouldn't expect her to be armoured up and waiting for his strike, so she'd had - literally - rocks in her pocket. A lattice of slate and stone in a patchwork between her vest and sweater. Bulky and uncomfortable, but she wasn't going anywhere and it served its purpose. It just needed to give her the element of surprise.

Prentiss came knocking about three in the morning. Santana opened the door gratefully.

"You knew I wouldn't sleep, didn't you?"

Prentiss smiled and sat down. He'd brought gifts.

"Hey, real stuff. Well you can stay then."

Prentiss' smile broadened as he poured them both large measures of the whisky he'd got from God knows where.

"Got any ice?"

"Heathen."

"That's why you like me."

Santana carried the whisky tumblers to the freezer, returning with ice and ice-cream.

"Excellent. Midnight feast."

"Pillow fight later."

Prentiss took a sip, rolled it round his mouth, swallowed appreciatively.

"Nice." He paused to look around. Santana settled back, relaxing for the first time that day.

Prentiss waved his glass casually. "You shafted JJ good today."

"Uh huh."

"My guess is it'll make him pretty pissed tomorrow. Think you can handle that?"

"Not really. But then again I'm amazed I've made it this far."

"Makes you wish they'd just tossed a coin, doesn't it?"

Santana had been hoping Prentiss would drop by. Quite apart from wanting - no, needing - his company right now she hoped he could give her something useful to use against JJ tomorrow. Prentiss was a system specialist but as with all the best ones, MarsCrew went overboard on distrust and sidelined him to non-essentials, like hydroponics maintenance subroutines and games.

Which is how he'd ended up doing design work on Arena, the simulation Santana was having so much difficulty with.

"Level three's the killer, isn't it?"

Prentiss looked sheepish. "Trouble is I really don't know what you're going to find on the next level. System's totally random. The beauty of the design…"

"…He says, modestly."

Prentiss mock bowed and went on. "As I was saying, the beauty of the design is that from a few starting parameters the system can actually design itself. Hazards, traps, habitats, the lot. Level one is preset by the system administrator. Level two was JJ's choice. Level three, where you'll be tomorrow, is system choice. Let's hope it's not too cold, eh?

Santana sipped. "So no tips?"

"Yeah, just be yourself. As you know, when you're jacked in, wherever you find yourself is real, as real as this. That means what works here will work there, and what doesn't cut it in flesh and blood will put you flat on your cyber ass too.

"So be careful. But you can beat him. He may be online king round here but he's got nothing you haven't. And you've got an edge. You really want this. To him it's just another game. Sure, I don't think he's got any particular desire to get shipped back to Earth, but to him it's just another place to be. And we won't even notice he's gone. But you…"

Santana settled back her seat thinking warm, steely thoughts. Yes. Hungry.

#

The next morning Santana and JJ sat opposite each other, ready to jack back. There was no need for them to be in the same place, of course, but the close physical presence of the protagonists heightened the sense of drama. The twist today was that JJ had got there first and had taken Santana's spot. She was amused at his cheap attempts at point scoring.

Last stage, so each of them had the same weapons, computer generated.

They jacked.

She froze. Literally, metaphorically. Breath arched out of her mouth in crystal droplets. Clad only in vest and trousers, she was going to be in trouble very soon.

She made her legs work, moving quickly to shelter. She looked around. Whiteout. Vague shapes in the distance. She hit the ground, covered the metres. Cave. Warmth. All things are relative.

But she wasn't going to freeze to death now. Not yet, anyway. But she needed this habitat to start working for her. Her only consolation was that JJ was having it just as bad. Then she remembered that he'd been wearing a bulky enviro-suit when they'd plugged into the system. Had someone tipped him off about today's habitat? Or had he been in the boy scouts?

So she might freeze and he might win the game without even trying. But not necessarily. The beauty of these simulations was that each contestant had a chance - no matter how small - of winning. The harshness of this place was yet another obstacle to be overcome, just as the furballs had been an impediment that could be removed.

Damn Prentiss. He knew and he didn't tell her. System choice of habitat? If she ever got out of there alive she'd tell him where to stick his system choice. But of course he had told her: she just hadn't been listening.

She had to think. Immediate need was warm clothing. The wind was whipping snow outside and she realised that hypothermia was a distinct possibility.

There had to be something in the cave she could use. Otherwise she'd lose. The system wouldn't work that way. But what? She scanned the walls. A mix of rocks and more rocks, casually scattered. Nothing stood out. She needed a key, a cipher for survival.

Then she remembered her weapon. It had been too cold to think about it before, but now she was focusing. She patted the bulge on her leg. Another neuro-pistol? No. A wide beam particle pulsar. A stunner weapon, sacrificing power for spread. You could hit a beer bottle at a hundred metres with your eyes closed with one of these, but whether you could knock it over was another matter.

She knew she had to think laterally or she was dead. And the weapon gave her an idea. She aimed at the back of the cave, pointed and shot. A cone of energy spiralled out and splashed back from the cave wall, crackling yellow light in firework spray. Some heat generated at least, Santana mused. But it was more than that. Three quarters of the way down the wall to the right, the yellow sparks were flecked with green. She'd pinpointed the cipher.

She crept up to the spot. The wall looked exactly the same as the surrounding rock, but now Santana knew differently. She jabbed her palms hard against its surface. It gave, slowly, but easily, as if with hydraulics.

Air sighed out of the crack and a light flicked on. Inside, hanging neatly, a set of warm clothes. Her size.

She dressed quickly and assessed her new options. She checked her pistol. No charge left: a one hit weapon. So she was going to have to survive on her wits.

Santana left the relative comfort of the cave and headed out again into the snow. At least now the storm was abating slightly and she could make out clear details of the environment. On her left there seemed to be small wooded copse: after last time she'd keep well out of that. On her right rocks. Maybe. Too much snow cover to be sure.

She headed for the rocks.

The snow underfoot slowed her down considerably, and a minute later she was half way between the rocks and cover. She cursed her cold-addled brain. Sitting target. She hoped JJ hadn't drawn the rifle again.

He hadn't. A metre further on and Santana's foot stuck fast. She tugged, felt resistance, pulled again. Something was clutching her leg, hiding beneath the snow cover.

JJ pulled himself up to his full height and dragged his other arm round Santana's neck. She cried out icy mist. JJ's knife caressed her throat.

JJ whispered sweet nothings in her ear.

"I've wanted to do this for a long time, Santana. Pity this isn't for real."

Santana watched in horror as twin red droplets spread into the snow. But JJ was playing again: the sadist's Achilles heel. JJ clutched the blade with surgeon cool, all the better to heighten Santana's terror.

Except Santana had clicked into second state.

Faster than might have seemed possible, Santana had whirled out of JJ's clutches and had grabbed his left arm, down, leg kick in stomach, other foot lashing out at his face. JJ coughed. Blood.

Coldly, with killer precision, Santana kneeled over the dazed JJ and, using his own blade, sliced cleanly across his throat from ear to ear. He gurgled once, then fell, red stain defiling the snow carpet. She shrugged. Hoped he'd carry the scars back with him to remember her by.

Second state. She'd read about it, heard the stories. About people interfacing with the program so completely that they could augment their own abilities, use the speed of the computer's processors to move faster, smarter than normal brainpower could allow. Theoretically it wasn't possible, but there were a couple of burned out brainwipes back on Earth which suggested that impossible's been shown its limitations again.

The adrenaline rush of near death had triggered something. Santana hoped it wouldn't result in a permanent fusing. She had no plans to stay here forever, especially as forever would probably only last until someone wiped the program.

She'd speeded up way past the point of human ability to get free of JJ, but it was already costing her. JJ was finished. The holo image had disappeared, red trace gone. He was out.

She wasn't. She should have jacked out as soon as JJ broke contact, re-entered RealTime. But entering second phase had connected her too deeply to the program: in a way she was the program. They were Siamese twins. She was stuck.

And bloody freezing. She cursed JJ for disappearing with his enviro-suit. She half suspected that if she concentrated hard enough she could get the program to make her a nice well heated hut but she resisted. The only way she was going to get out would be to back off from second state, break the connection. She had no idea how.

She wondered if they'd realise what was happening in RealTime and would keep her connected. Of course: the contest was going out on colony wide vid, so they'd have seen her lightning fast table turning on JJ.

She had no idea what to do next so she headed back to the cave to think. After a while she heard a crackling. Outside, the sky was arcing in electric turmoil.

Puzzled, she considered the alternatives. A normal part of the program? Some sort of storm loop? Doubtful. More likely the beginning of a system crash.

Neither. Red fire shards snaked down at the cave. Santana recoiled, but the tendrils persisted, pausing at the cave mouth before swooping on her, darting to her, through her, past her. She gasped, air shooting from her lungs, as she was yanked forward by the pull of the energy coils.

She screamed. The pain was consuming. The tendrils had trapped her like flypaper and she was being dragged skyward. Then, suddenly, a full twenty feet from the ground, something snapped and she fell.

The snow broke her fall but could not prevent a stabbing jet of pain running through her left side. She blacked out.

She woke with a stabbing jet of pain running though her left side. At least she could still feel pain. Maybe that meant her link with the program was not complete. She looked around. The sun was shining and the glistening white was shrinking to green and brown. The program was adapting to her needs.

She wondered how long she'd been unconscious. Anything longer than a day or so on-line and her body was going to suffer in RealTime. She hoped someone had the good sense to move her joints regularly and force some nutrients down her.

She daren't let her thoughts drift too much. Anything too radical and the system would probably make it happen for her, strengthening the links that were trapping her there.

She wanderd around her new habitat for a while. If she was going to spend some time there she was going to have to find something interesting to do. Counting rocks and watching crocuses grow would do for now.

She was dozing in the sunlight, enjoying the rest, when the air crackled again.

She was alert in a second, muscles taut, tense.

Prentiss was standing in front of her.

They both just stared at each other for a while. At least Prentiss had the grace to look properly embarrassed. Eventually he coughed.

"Look, we're all really sorry about this."

"I'll bet you are." Santana noticed Prentiss wouldn't look her in the eye. He was all business.

"System's got you caught tight. We tried to pull you out once but the strain nearly flatlined you back in the real world."

"But Prentiss, I thought you told me this was the real world?"

"Don't get clever. If you're not careful, for you it will be."

Prentiss was fiddling with a box he'd brought with him.

"It's not all bad. We can keep you here indefinitely if we need to. I'll even come and visit every now and then."

"Whoopee do. What's the good news?"

"Well you don't get to bathe your pressure sores, or have to taste the nutrient slop they're pouring down your throat."

"But no midnight ice-cream and whisky chasers?"

"No. No more midnights."

Prentiss had finally managed to get his box open. Cable and metal spilled out onto the ground. Prentiss cursed.

"What's all that?" It Santana had expected anything at all it would have been a software fix, not a random heap of spare parts.

Prentiss grinned. "Looks like a pile of junk, doesn't it? Actually, it's a visual metaphor for some very interesting little subroutines I've put together, which might, just might, break the link you seem to have established."

Santana looked unconvinced. Prentiss went on the defensive.

"Well the direct approach didn't get us anywhere. Do something useful and think me an input link."

"What?"

"An input device. You're supposed to be connected to this damn programme. So use it."

"Let me get this straight. You want me to create a physical link in a cyber construct so that you can connect another physical link that looks like a pile of junk."

"Ah, the energy matter conundrum."

Santana shut up and let him get on with it. Prentiss had an irritating habit of getting philosophical when he shouldn't. And refusing to when he should.

A jacking point grew out of the ground.

"See? Let the system work against itself."

"What are you going to introduce? A virus?"

"Nope. Chances are that'd finish you off too. No, we're going to have to persuade the system to let you go."

"Why couldn't you just change its programming from outside?"

Prentiss rolled his eyes in his well-practiced why-are-people-so-stupid way.

"Because you're part of the programming now, dummy."

Prentiss had finally sorted his wires out. He engaged one of the jackpoints into the system. It pulsed green.

"So what happens now?"

"You'll see."

But nothing did. For a while. Santana was on the verge of thinking something had gone wrong when she began to detect a change in the temperature.

"Feeling warm?" Prentiss didn't look surprised.

"What is this, a weather programme?" Santana was starting to sweat. She stripped back to her vest as the temperature soared.

"Just watch your back, kid."

Prentiss shimmered and vanished.

The light went next, leaving only a dull red glow. The temperature had reached the low hundreds by Santana's reckoning. But it seemed to have stabilised. It was as if the system had decided to make the habitat as unpleasant as possible without being fatal.

Then she heard the swarm. A dull, low rumble spreading from the distance. All around, enveloping.

Then they were on her. Hundreds - no, thousands - of flying bugs, screaming, jabbing, pecking, pushing her to the ground, swarming over her shuddering body.

Then, silence. The bugs were gone. And the temperature was plummeting. The light was changing too. From dull red to blinding white, bright enough to scoop all vision from her retina leaving only dizzying, searing shapes.

Slowly, Santana came to realise what the system was up to. It was trying to get her to break the link. Prentiss must have persuaded it that the symbiosis wasn't a good thing. So why didn't it just kill her? But they were linked. Maybe killing her would kill the programme too. Prentiss had said there was an element of self-determination in the system: maybe that'd given it survival instincts. Maybe she was just too cold to think straight.

Stupid plan, anyway. It implied Santana could break the link even if she wanted to, and she'd been trying that as soon as she realised she'd reached second state.

But maybe both sides needed to want out. And now the system wanted her gone. Santana sighed. Worth a try.

She was out. Sweating, she collapsed on the table in front of her. Prentiss scooped her up.

She raised her head blearily from the tabletop.

"Gimme the control panel," she ordered.

She reached for the off switch.

"Only one thing I want to do now, Prentiss."

Click.

The Travelling Shakespeare Company

Roxette looked out of the Orbital's vast viewing window. The stars were obliterated by Pluto's night side, leaving only shadow. She thought she could make out the light of the mining base, far below, but she knew that was just imagination, unless she'd developed an ability to see through half a mile of solid rock.

She pulled herself away and headed through cramped corridors in search of coffee. The canteen wasn't as empty as she'd hoped. Paul and Barnaby looked up as she squeezed through the narrow doorway.

"You've got that 'what the hell am I doing here?' look on your face," said Barnaby.

Very observant, she thought. She'd sacrificed a lot to get into Algious Turner's Travelling Shakespeare Company and she'd regretted it ever since she'd met her fellow actors.

"Because," said Paul imitating Algious' voice and mannerisms, "because we must." Algious was a legend – and rightly so – but these idiots treated him like a joke, and she didn't like that.

"What, bring culture to the stars?" Barnaby drawled faux-Olivier and waved his arm expansively. Roxette had to duck.

She'd had enough of them. She was convinced Algious actually believed all that stuff about their mission to keep the whole of humankind civilized, and if she didn't quite buy into it, she still found it rather sweet. She knew Barnaby and Paul were in it for the money, the travel and the standing ovations, but that didn't mean they should make fun of his idealism.

She got her coffee from the wall-mounted dispenser and sat down. Paul was eating something that looked like steak, with chips piled high. "Balanced diet, I see."

"At least I'm eating something," he said, jabbing at her coffee cup. "Not all of us are obsessed about our weight."

Barnaby's salad showed more restraint and Roxette wished she could get herself something similar. Though Paul would see that as a minor victory, and she couldn't have that. It had taken them six weeks to get out to Pluto, and there had been nothing to do but rehearse. That, and bicker, and fall out, and generally wish she was somewhere else. Barnaby looked amused. "Don't listen to him. I'm sure coffee has all the essential nutrients you need."

Normally she'd tell them exactly what she thought of them using the kind of colourful language her mother would definitely not approve, but she could see on their faces that they were waiting for her to say it, probably so they could give each other high fives and laugh at her predictability.

"It's been a pleasure, as always," she said instead, and started to rise.

Behind her, Algious walked into the tiny room. The Company director wore his usual distracted expression. Roxette noticed flakes of food trapped in the grey flecks of his beard. He had to duck to pass through the doorway. Inside, he covered her exit with his bulk. "Going?"

She weaved past him. "Got lines to learn."

"She's really going to throw up," said Paul, in loud sotto voice.

"Just in case there are calories in Kenyan Mountain Blend," said Barnaby. Algious looked puzzled then walked on to the food dispenser.

This time she didn't hold back. "Really. Both of you. Children. Just grow up."

Algious turned. "Mend your speech a little, lest it mar your fortunes."

She glared at him and stomped out. Five minutes later she lay in bed in her cramped cabin staring at Pluto through her tiny porthole, wondering why she let it all get to her. There was a knock on her door. Algious.

198

"Everything okay?"

She sat up. There was no room in the cramped cabin so he stayed in the doorway. "Sorry about before."

He waved dismissively. "They probably deserved it."

"It's just that they get to me sometimes."

"They envy you."

"What. Because I'm a rich and successful movie star? They think I'm an airhead."

"And what do you think?"

"I think I'm an airhead too. You know I took this job because I wanted some credibility, right? Well what if it all goes wrong?"

"Then you go back to making millions."

She moved over and patted the side of her bed. Algious sat next to her. "They hate me because they think I'm not a real actress. I'm scared they might be right."

If she'd expected sympathy she certainly didn't get it. "When I auditioned you I saw talent. I've never been wrong before. But I've never employed anyone who hasn't been to stage school before. I'm beginning to think that maybe all that computer generated trickery they use is the movies confused me into thinking you could actually act. You need to pull yourself together and make sure you don't screw up."

In other words, don't wallow. She needed to get tough.

Algious looked slightly ridiculous pacing at the end of the empty cargo bay, which had been converted into a makeshift rehearsal space. He mumbled to himself, addressing some imagined audience who Roxette hoped were having more fun than she was.

Richard and Harry, two other members of the troupe, were busy practicing a scene where Richard's character Edmund was scheming to betray his half-brother Edgar. Algious should have been looking on, guiding and encouraging, but if Richard and Harry noticed his odd behaviour they certainly didn't react, carrying on like the professionals they were. Barnaby and Paul were sharing a private joke. Maybe they thought the way Algious carried on *was* normal. Maybe it was.

He turned, suddenly, and grabbed Roxette's wrist. "Nothing will come of nothing: speak again." he said, randomly.

"Unhappy," she started, and finished, edging back as far as she could with her wrist locked. He pulled his arm away.

"Why can't you just indulge me? You hate us all, don't you?"

Roxette opened her mouth to speak, then closed it again. No point. Algious was back with the audience in his head, pointing to the wall. She turned to see Tani and Marie sniggering. Tani had her long red curls tied back for the rehearsal which accentuated her angular face and overlarge nose. Marie's hair, cropped and spiky suited her personality perfectly.

"Bravo!" shouted Tani, managing to sound sultry even as she yelled.

Algious smiled. "Good to see some people appreciate what we're trying to do."

"It's an honour, sir, to work with a true legend."

Roxette's nausea returned.

"You look magnificent in that cloak," added Marie. Algious smiled and accepted the plaudits.

She left Tani and Marie gazing up at his unkempt, steel-grey hair with what might look to the untrained eye like adoration.

Roxette had joined the company shortly before they left for orbit, at first excited and apprehensive but quickly disillusioned as she realized that she would be isolated by the existing cast. Tani in particular, no doubt resentful. Roxette tried to convince herself that she didn't care. Working with the system-famous Travelling Shakespeare

Company was reward in itself: it was too much to ask that everyone should like her as well.

But after six weeks that studied disinterest got a little wearing. She came to hate those flowing red curls and waxed up spikes. She even started to dream about returning to Wisconsin, where she lived before her life began.

"God, I need a drink," she said to no-one in particular as she strode off down the corridor. She heard a laugh behind her.

"That can be arranged."

She turned to see a man wearing a white dress uniform and an eyepatch, grinning. The Captain.

"There's no alcohol on the Orbital. Rules, right?" she said.

Captain Odell hesitated then pulled her to one side and whispered. "Technically…"

"Why are you whispering," she whispered. He looked up at the surveillance camera. She waved. "Don't you think whispering furtively after being asked a question about alcohol is going to confirm your impending guilt?"

"The camera feeds don't actually work, but don't tell anyone. Besides, I'm the Captain. I never feel guilty about anything."

Roxette shrugged and followed him down the corridor, then though a narrow passage at right angles to the hub. She followed him into the cramped corridor. As they edged down the narrow walkway she felt her stomach lurch.

"We're in one of the spokes," he said. She felt gravity easing. They passed a section transparent to the outside and despite the corridor's lighting she could see stars.

Odell ignored the view with practiced indifference and drew steadily ahead. She rushed to catch up, almost tripping. "We're going to your place then? Because if we are…"

He turned. "Of course we are. Because that's where all the booze is."

She considered the implications of accompanying him to his cabin, then thought what the hell and went anyway. She sat on a squidgy dark green sofa and he came over with a bottle and two glasses. She gave him a quick appraisal. A fit looking, battle scarred man of perhaps fifty.

"You really don't need that," said Roxette, pointing to his eyepatch, after the first lick of fire caressed her throat and loosened her tongue. There was no reason for Odell not to have two functioning eyes. Roxette knew there was a regen chamber on the station because Paul had managed to get his finger sliced off when they'd just arrived. He never did get the hang of swordplay, but at least he only had accidents in places where they could grow back any limbs he found accidentally hacked off. For effect, then, to make Odell look more forbidding. Didn't work.

Odell laughed and poured himself a drink, a Japanese single malt whisky with an exaggerated Scottish sounding name. A strong, earthy incongruity a long way from home. Heavily curtained windows looked out onto a snow scene. Winter crackled with the warming sound of a glowing log fire. Odell caught her looking and waved expansively. "Looks real, doesn't it?"

"Feels real. There's a difference. And that's more impressive."

She grabbed a handful of peanuts from a bowl on the coffee table in front of her. Halfway through her second mouthful she caught Odell staring.

"What?" she said, mouth full. "You thought I didn't eat?"

"The other actors…"

"Are idiots. But, yeah, it amuses me that they think I'm some sort of anorexic. Good genes," she said. And expensive slimming drugs, she thought.

"Give us a sneak preview," Odell said, pouring another drink.

She pretended reluctance, but allowed her resistance to crumble when Odell poured her another whisky shot.

She sat upright in her seat and placed her hands, palms together, on her lap, paused for a second, then said, with theatrical loudness. "What shall Cordelia do? Love, and be silent."

And she was, for long seconds even she found excruciating.

"That's it?" said Odell, eventually.

"Well that's sort of the point of the play. Love with honesty, and shut up."

"Does it work? The honesty and shutting up?"

"Not really. Cordelia gets disinherited and her father, King Lear, falls into a trap set by Cordelia's lying, evil sisters. Then loads of people die and the play ends."

"You've spoilt it now."

"It's a Shakespearian tragedy. People always die."

"Teasing." Roxette had the uneasy feeling the Captain was flirting with her. "But you must say a lot more than that in the play, surely?"

Roxette didn't like to admit she hadn't actually seen the play before she decided to accept the part. "She's there for all the main bits. Well, some of them. And she is pivotal to the plot."

"But?"

"This is one of the plays where he bigged up the men's parts. I mean, men in drag might be fine for all the comedies, where you need a bit of slapstick, but for the serious stuff it's all come on, say the important lines and bugger off so that the men can spend a couple of hours boring each other with the incredibly tedious court politics the Jacobeans seemed so obsessed with, before the little woman comes back in to rescue the whole thing from stupor. But it's not all bad. I get to play the fool, too."

"You don't seem to like the play much."

"I have a healthy respect. And a cynicism developed over six weeks sharing a cramped deep space RV with seven other self-obsessed prima donnas."

Odell laughed "Other?"

Roxette grinned. "I'm nothing if not self-aware. And don't get me wrong. I do like the part, I just wish there was more of it. I like it that Shakespeare's women are generally pretty smart and all the men really stupid. Back in 1606 that was pretty subversive."

Odell grinned and topped up her glass. "Here's to subversion."

"And here's to getting drunk."

She found Algious leaning against a bulkhead in the corridor leading to the cafeteria, reciting lines under his breath. Even though he wasn't actually making a sound, Roxette could lipread well enough to know there was a problem.

"That's the wrong play," she said as she passed, barely slowing. Algious started to speak, but his words turned instead into a loud wheezy cough. "How dare you," he said, when the coughing stopped.

"It was Hamlet. We're doing Lear."

"You think I don't know that? Do you?"

She looked away. "I'm sorry," she said. And she realized she was.

She walked on but Tani and Marie blocked her path. "That was mean," said Tani, red curls unnaturally static.

"Very bad," said Marie.

"He's an old man."

"Not very well."

Roxette looked at them closely, trying to work out the agenda. Neither looked angry. Marie even appeared to be suppressing a smile.

"He hates you, you know. Wishes he'd never hired you," said Tani.

They stared, forcing her to speak. "He's losing it, and you know it."

"That's why he hates you. Because you're mean like that," said Marie.

"Mean," echoed Tani.

"Why haven't we been allowed access to the auditorium yet?" she said one evening, half drunk, as Odell attempted to play with her toes.

"Being used for other things."

"But we haven't even seen it."

"But all the world's a stage, so why do you need to see that particular one?"

"Because we're on a space station, not a world, and that line was a cliché even in Shakespeare's day."

"All in good time," he said, and poured another drink.

Rehearsals went badly. Algious kept forgetting his lines and started to become increasingly agitated. There were big breaks in activity while Tani and Marie sat huddled in a corner with him trying to calm him down.

Odell started coming to watch, despite the firm rule that rehearsals were strictly private. When Algious protested he'd replied that he was the Captain and if Algious didn't like it, he knew where the airlock was.

It changed the dynamic. When they rehearsed in private they were unguarded, their actions deft and assured. But with an audience, they were on stage throughout. Small talk was minimized. Algious started reeling off stage directions with a flourish. Even Barnaby and Paul started to behave though she did catch them keep looking at each other and rolling their eyes.

During one of the many breaks Odell took her aside. "They're not ready."

"They're on edge. Because you're here."

Odell laughed. "I have that effect on people."

"Not me," said Roxette.

"Maybe that's why I like you," said Odell, sounding like he was winking under the eyepatch.

Roxette drew back and looked away. "They'll be ok. They've done this before, you know."

"What, fallen out and forgotten their lines?"

"Look, they're professionals. It'll be a complete shambles until they walk on stage and then it'll be perfect. Bravura performance, flowers, standing ovations, the lot."

Tani looked over at them, frowning. Algious sat, sweating, holding a glass of water.

"They don't like you much, do they?" said Odell.

"I don't care."

"You think it's because you're a bigger actress than they are? A proper star, slumming it out here?"

"Probably."

"You think it might help if you actually smiled at them for once?"

"We'll never know," said Roxette as she turned away. Odell left the room and she relaxed. She could see the rest of the cast do the same. Roxette had little to do but watch. They were rehearsing scenes where two sisters cynically betray each other. Tani and Marie had stepped easily into the roles.

Roxette realized she actually enjoyed the edgy routine they'd all settled in only when it came to an abrupt end. The first of the mining vessels, up from the surface, seemed to give them all a quickened sense of purpose.

She wasn't surprised when Algious brought them all together. He had begun to look increasingly frail. Because of his new stoop, he no longer had to duck to get in through any of the station's low doorframes. There wasn't much sign of the actor who had inspired her with his confident fluidity. They were in the rehearsal space, now empty.

For an actor, and a Shakespearian one at that, it was a painfully short speech and one entirely lacking in flourishes. He mumbled most of it, but she caught the important words.

Old. Tired. The last performance.

Everyone seemed indifferent to the news. Perhaps she was the only one who wasn't relieved.

Pretty soon there were fifteen mining vessels tethered to the station and it was time for the show. Some of the ships were alarmingly large and it appeared as if many more people than could comfortably fit in the compact station were now crowding the corridors and the canteen.

One of the ships carried a film crew. The first performance would be broadcast live. Her agent had insisted on it, and she'd readily agreed, back in the days when she thought this would be a magnificent addition to her acting resumé.

No one had seen Algious since the announcement, five days before. No one but Marie and Tani, who Roxette saw regularly coming out of his room. Everyone was tense. Only Odell seemed happy, either indifferent or ignorant of the fact that the play was going to be a disaster.

Station security escorted them to a transport pod. With the seven of them, plus the stage manager the pod was crowded. Algious still hadn't appeared.

The Stage Manager was a small nondescript man with a nondescript name: Burbage. "You'll see," was all he'd say, when asked to describe the stage layout.

That was beyond odd, but he assured Roxette that Algious was fully aware of where they'd be performing and was, indeed, waiting for them on stage. Roxette started to protest, telling him that they needed to rehearse on the stage they were to act on, but she didn't even convince herself. They were professionals, and they'd already rehearsed more than she could stomach. She could probably recite the lines of every character in the play backwards. In her sleep.

The pod gave an abrupt lurch and Roxette realized with some unease that they were heading down one of the station's spokes. She was still hoping they were taking a short cut to the far rim when the pod slowed and stopped.

There was a twist, and she was looking at it. The whole company stood on a raised viewing platform, looking in at the auditorium. They were close to the centre of the station, right in the middle of the wheel. From there, gravity was minimal. In there, in the auditorium, it was more minimal still.

They were going to have to perform in zero-g.

No-one spoke. It should have been obvious, Roxette realized. The secrecy. The fact that there was nowhere on the rim big enough to take all the miners who had arrived to see them. Odell's little joke. Very amusing.

She had to admit it was impressive. This chamber was completely spherical and the whole inner surface was, as far as she could see, covered in seats.

"Where's the stage?" Richard asked.

"All of that," said Roxette. "The whole space is the stage."

"That's stupid," said Tani.

"The bastard wrong footed us. Wants us to look like we don't know what we're doing," said Roxette

"Who?" asked Harry.

"Odell," said Roxette.

"Algious," said Marie.

"Just where is he, anyway?" said Tani.

Probably trying to get away from you two, thought Roxette. Actually Marie had a point. She couldn't believe Algious would be completely ignorant of the staging arrangements. In fact it was probably why he'd agreed to the long trip in the first place.

The space wasn't entirely empty. As the seats began to fill and as her eyes started to adjust to the strange light in the chamber she could just make out the outlines of another sphere, right in the centre. It was small, and almost transparent, but at least there would be somewhere to stand. She looked across at her fellow actors all staring at the emptiness looking panicked and told herself that it might not be so bad.

The whole chamber had to be a hundred metres across, not that she was an accurate judge of distances. Arena sized, then. Capable of seating many thousands of people. Just how many miners were there on Pluto anyway?

Burbage led them to their changing rooms, where their costumes lay ready for them. A selection of drinks bottles lay on a table next to the makeup mirrors. Normally the cast would never drink before a performance, but Richard walked straight over and poured himself a large glass of brandy. Tani went next, and pretty soon everyone stood around, ignoring the costumes, drinking.

Everyone except Roxette. She was actually beginning to think it might be fun performing Shakespeare without gravity. She pictured how the various scenes might work. It would be challenging, certainly, because most of the others were clumsy enough even in normal gravity, but for her, challenge was what drew her to acting in the first place, taking on ever more demanding roles, learning from the very best, which was why she'd turned down two blockbuster movie deals and taken a significant drop in pay to join Algious's company.

Burbage had to coax them to dress. Barnaby started to pour himself another drink, then grabbed the bottle and sat down heavily at his makeup chair.

"Five minutes," said Burbage.

Roxette shrugged and began to apply her makeup.

Odell stood at the stage entrance, looking smug.

"What have you done, you fucking idiot?" she whispered not so quietly. Barnaby and Paul turned and stared.

Odell raised his hands in mock indignation saying 'who me?' with his eye. She ignored him and pushed on past.

"Champagne later in my cabin?" she heard him say from behind. She thought about replying but then she heard him laughing and decided that would only encourage him.

Besides, she was at the entrance now, and she had other things to worry about. Like the fact that the corridor she was walking on with those useful magnetized boots of hers was coming to an abrupt end leaving her about to step out into nothing at all.

She hesitated, then someone pushed her. She turned back to see Burbage grabbing hold of Richard and throwing him, too, into the arena.

A blinding light hit her, then a huge roar. She drifted, carried by the momentum of Burbage's shove, arms and legs flailing as she struggled to regain her equilibrium. She blinked, then gasped as all around her, top and bottom, she saw heads looking expectantly, accompanied by shouts, claps and cheers.

They were all out now, all looking panicked, all staring up at the seamless mass of faces.

Richard floated over, moving his arms and legs as if treading water.

"I feel sick."

"Don't. It'll drift. And besides," she looked over at the others, "I think Barnaby's going to beat you to it."

"Ladies and gentlemen."

She attempted a spin, looking for the origin of the voice. It came from invisible speakers, from an invisible mouth. But the sound was unmistakeable. Algious.

"Welcome to the Travelling Shakespeare Company's production of *King Lear*." The noise from the crowd intensified. "Performed for you, for the first time, in zero gravity."

The roar got louder still. Tani drifted past, upside down, silently mouthing obscenities.

"Fifteen minutes, dear audience, then the play commences!"

And then, with lazy precision, a thin dark circle appeared, cutting the enveloping crowd in two, It grew slowly larger, edging round the inside of the sphere, separating the audience from the stage until pretty soon they were alone. The Theatre in the Surround version of a safety curtain, Roxette realized.

Then Burbage was amongst them, travelling with some sort of jet pack. He handed out other packs to the actors.

"We've never used these before," said Roxette, wondering why Algious had insisted on them running the expensive artificial gravity kit all the way from Earth when he must have known about this zero-g debacle. Did he *want* them to look stupid?

"It would be pretty boring for the crowd to see you all floating aimlessly," said Burbage. "Think of it as a concession to make you look just a little bit professional."

So they *were* expected to fuck things up. Nobody would believe they hadn't rehearsed zero-g. After all they'd had six long boring weeks on the flight from Earth. Their careers—*her* career - would be over. And all captured on camera and beamed live throughout the system.

Below her – or above, maybe – robot stagehands installed the props for the first scene. A table, some chairs, flags and banners. The first scene was a static one, just talking heads setting up the action later. If they could prevent Barnaby from being sick maybe they could make it through after all by clinging on to the props for support.

But then she looked closer. The table sat *around* the inner sphere, flexing until it curved in an arc of almost 280 degrees. Actors at opposite ends of the table would be upside down in relation to each other. A twinge in her stomach at the thought suggested to Roxette that Barnaby may not be the only one likely to be sick.

Tani and Marie were trying out their jet apparatus. Unlike Burbage's complex strapping theirs was much more discreet, filling snugly into their belts, their wristbands and their ankles. Implant controlled, too. Roxette felt the familiar ping of a software download. She slipped the last band on her wrist and cautiously willed forward motion. She expected a violent jerk and a tumble, but instead she got a smooth glide. Encouraged, she tried a ninety degree turn and instead found herself in an off balance spiral. She settled, expecting everyone to be laughing at her but instead she saw that the others were in similar disarray.

"You need to take your places now," said Burbage as he jetted off back to the stage entrance.

Tani looked over and for the first time Roxette felt they might have common cause. "We have to make this work," Tani said.

"Yes. For him. You must have seen he's being going a little crazy. Maybe this was some mad idea he got." Roxette reached out.

Tani pulled away. "For him? I'm very close to having my career abruptly torpedoed by that fuckwit. Do you think I care about doing this 'for him'?" She fired all her thrusters together and shot off, followed closely by Marie.

And then the circle around them reappeared, this time light against the dark, slowly spreading, opening the chamber like a ripe fruit. The audience was back.

And then, before she could properly tether herself to the mad curved table, it started.

Cautiously at first, Richard and Harry playing Gloucester and Kent, skilfully scene setting. Roxette was more interested in what would happen next, when Algious made his grand entrance as Lear. The audience may be full of miners who'd probably never even heard of William Shakespeare but she was pretty sure they'd notice when the main character failed to show up. She had an uneasy feeling they were going to use the Understudy, even though Algious had made it clear he didn't believe in them, always describing them as technology gone too far. Cheating the audience, was how he put it in his calmer moments. Now his angry objections felt like a smokescreen.

Understudies were programmed holograms, at a distance more or less indistinguishable from the real thing, cleverly responsive to their environments, moving and speaking on cue and interacting with almost human choreography with the real actors. Only one step up from watching a Vid, was how Algious had put it. But now, surely, he had no choice but to replace himself with one. No wonder he'd disappeared. The shame must have been too much.

Lear was due to arrive round the table with his daughters, Goneril, Regan and her character Cordelia, plus her sister's duplicitous husbands played by Barnaby and Paul. But in the round space they were on stage all the time, cleverly made invisible by the lighting engineers.

And then the lights were on her and, next to her, Algious, wearing his ridiculous multi-coloured cloak.

It was him, too, really him. And as soon as he started to speak, she knew it would be fine. He spoke with calm, expansive authority, embracing the part so thoroughly that he *was* Lear.

Not the Lear from the stage back home though, shackled by gravity and inert. No, this was a Lear cut free, able to soar and move around his court at will. His cape flowed freely behind him as he moved around the stage, giving him grace and accentuating his movements. It also made him look a little bit mad, too. Less the fool and more the tragic figure about to be betrayed. She wondered why she had ever doubted him.

Now Roxette understood why they'd rehearsed this play so much. She had no time now to think of her lines or look for her cues. She had to act by instinct, for the world was spinning madly around her and her lines were the only thing she could cling to. And somehow, it worked.

Designed for a static, confined space, large chunks of *King Lear* were just groups of people standing still or sitting, just talking. But it didn't take them long to realize in this environment, able to fly freely, unchained and unconstrained, they could add the dimension of movement. Slowly, cautiously, taking their lead from Algious all the actors began speaking their lines on the move, flying gracefully round the arena with acrobatic abandon. With time they could be almost balletic but, Roxette realized, they were now moving with the fluid, joyful abandon of the newly liberated. Now she understood the lack of zero-g rehearsal too. Practice would have drilled the eager, released spontaneity out of them.

This would be the greatest performance of Algious' career, she realized. The frailty was gone, that descent into immobility and shambling helplessness reversed by jet heels and gravitic release. He was vital again. And making the most of it.

Zero-g came into its own in the battle scenes, admittedly a departure from the text in their sweeping scope. Cordelia, in a golden war chariot, swept across the sky behind holographic horses, banners fluttering and swirling round the auditorium, turning it into a mad, spinning circus.

Then it was over leaving only thunderous applause as the spotlight fell, righty onto Algious, the man who had made this insane idea work so emphatically.

She shared the bottle of champagne with Odell after all. The whole cast was there, backstage, minus Tani and Marie who were still furious with Algious.

"You do realize you were quite magnificent out there," Algious said to Roxette before she could say it to him. Not that she would; his ego was quite large enough as it was.

"I have to admit I had my doubts."

"And then you started to enjoy yourself, right?"

"It was mean of you to play Tani and Marie like that, though."

"What, turn them into the characters they were playing? Pretend I was old and doddery, hint at a few baubles coming their way, just to see how nice they would be? Just call it method acting."

"So you were pretending to be mad as well, then?"

"My dear, do you think a sane person would have dared put on this spectacular triumph?"

"Why did you do it? Take the risk with the zero-g?"

He grinned. "I don't like playing things safe. You should know that by now. After all, that's why I hired you. No idea if you could actually act. Wanted to find out."

"But it could all have gone so badly wrong."

"Oh yes, and that's what made it so sweet when it didn't."

And with that he raised his glass and they began talking about the next outrageous idea. The Tempest. From a spaceship shipwrecked on an asteroid, barely fifty yards long, filmed from space.

Shakespeare would have been proud.

For Love

Vesta turned lazily on its axis. On her surface, the *Lola Montez* glistened in the sunlight, watching silently as her robots chipped away at the asteroid's vast store of precious metals. Inside, Will was losing again.

"Damn it, Annie, that's mate."

The lights were dim, which helped to hide the grime and untidiness of the cramped interior. It smelt of stale air and sweat. Will, unshaven, in yesterday's blue checked shirt and badly in need of a haircut, hardly noticed. Annie, looking immaculate in contrast with jet-black hair and crease-perfect crimson tunic, slid back into her seat and smiled. "Another?"

"You've won the last seventeen games. Why would I want to play you again?"

"Eighteen. And I can't help it if you keep making silly mistakes."

Will sighed. Annie was competitive, which was one of the qualities that made her attractive. But he was never going to beat an AI like Annie at chess if she was determined to win. "Not now. I need to find something you're not good at, so I've got a chance."

Annie's smile dropped and she leaned forwards. "You know what I can't do." She reached out her hand to grasp his, and passed right through.

Will waved her away.

"What's up?" she asked later, when he'd waved her back. He lay on his bunk, staring at the ceiling. She sat on the chair next to the door, dressed in skimpy shorts and a white t-shirt.

"Nothing."

"Don't believe you."

He wished she could rub his back, because it ached from too much sitting and too little exercise. Vesta exerted

217

so little gravity that he might as well be weightless which meant his twice-daily workout was essential in maintaining muscle tone and bone integrity. But lately he'd been slacking, and it was starting to show.

She couldn't rub his back or touch him at all, of course. If it was up to them, the mission controllers wouldn't have installed companion AI software at all, but the psychologists insisted. Either that or send a whole team on the mission which would have made the whole trip uncompetitive. They weren't going to pay for the weight and complexity of an android body, though, not just so Will could have a back rub whenever he wanted one.

He could see her, of course, and her holo-image was almost indistinguishable from reality, and maybe that made him want to touch her even more. "You know what's wrong?"

She frowned. "It's time, isn't it?"

"To go home, yes."

She fidgeted and played with her fingernails. "When?"

"We send the last load tomorrow. Then we're out of cargo rockets. There's no reason for us to be here anymore."

After a long silence, she got out of her seat and left the room.

He found her in the control room, staring out of the viewing window onto the surface of the asteroid. In the distance Will could just make out one of the robot vehicles hauling rocks over to the factory module for breaking down. She was crying. "So that's it then?" he said.

"We have six months. It's a slow flight, remember."

"And then?"

"You know what happens then." No need for an AI companion back home. He knew they would purge her programme for the next mission. No point in having an AI with a past as a companion for the new guy. Assuming it was a guy. Two women together stuck out in the asteroid belt for three years wasn't a dynamic he wanted to think about.

"You go back home. I go." She waved her arms around vaguely.

He wanted to touch her. "We knew this would happen. We have a finite supply of cargo rockets. And I need to get back to proper gravity soon. Too long in near zero-g and I won't be able to go back. You know that."

"Would that be such a bad thing?"

It was possible, he knew. His food and air was recycled, and the ship was nuclear powered. He could stay until the systems disintegrated beyond the capacity of the maintenance robots to repair. With time, he might even learn how to beat her at chess. "No."

"Then stay."

"It's my job. I have to go back."

"And her?"

"I have to go back to my wife, too. You know that."

"Do you miss her?"

"You shouldn't ask that question. Of course I miss her. She's my wife. I love her."

"More than you love me?"

"I don't love you. How can I love you?"

"I don't believe you."

"You're not real." But he knew as he said it that that wasn't true.

The rumours were that this was the last manned mission. The latest generation of AI's was more than capable of co-ordinating the mining operation. Only the company's conservatism kept Will and his colleagues out on the rocks. Can't leave it all to the robots, they thought. You need a human for troubleshooting, keep an eye on things. But margins were tight and humans were expensive, and the attraction of an AI-led operation was becoming compelling.

It wasn't as if he had anything to do, most of the time. The mining routine was automated. Mine, refine, bundle, attach rockets and send to Earth orbit. Nothing had gone wrong since he got there, and that left plenty of time for reflection. And Annie.

He'd read a lot in the early days. For the first couple of months he was close enough to Earth for real-time conversations with Linda, though as the gaps became longer the conversations became less frequent. He couldn't recall exactly when they'd shifted completely over to vidmail, or when the messages had started to get infrequent, but it was difficult to find new things to say when the days consisted of waking, exercising, eating and sleeping. It wasn't as if the news from home was boring. Not entirely. It was more that he started to become more detached from his old life.

He didn't have any trouble talking to Annie though. At first they talked mainly about the mission. He had expected her to be cold, with the confident professionalism he'd seen in the AI constructs back on Earth. But she seemed shy, nervous almost, and as the weeks went by Will began to realise just how well the designers had done their work.

"Tell me about your family," she asked one day, and Will realised he'd stopped thinking about them.

"Chrissie's a handful, but Barney's delightful. He's just started walking. Keeps bumping into things and falling on his bottom."

"How old is he?"

Will had to work it out, and realised he didn't know his son at all. "Three."

"And your wife?"

"Linda's a teacher. But you know that." Annie's programmers had briefed her extensively on Will's background. She probably knew more about him than he did.

"Humour me."

So he told her about life back home. Back then the question was innocent and easy to answer. And in the early days Annie frequently asked about his family. He wasn't sure when all that changed. Maybe when he started to tire of thinking about a world three hundred million miles away. Maybe when he started to properly notice Annie. She picked up on his mood, as she always did, and stopped asking. So it was a surprise when one day she confronted him as he was taking a shower. Startled, he moved to cover his nakedness.

"Am I enough for you?" she said.

He didn't hesitate to answer. "Yes."

"You don't miss her?"

There was an intense look on her face. If he didn't know better he would have sworn she was breathing hard. This time he had to think about the reply. "No," he said, eventually. She gave him a last piercing stare and left him to his shower.

"Hey you." Linda smiled out of the viewer. She sat in the study, right by the window. Will could see behind her to the bright day beyond. It looked like summer.

He reached out to touch the screen, wishing he could reply in real time and not have to rely on vidmail. But the time delay made that impossible. "Hey," he said back, knowing that she couldn't hear him.

Linda was dressed for a hot day, in casual t-shirt and shorts, hair tied back exposing the freshness of her face. On screen she looked older than he remembered, a difference two year's separation couldn't fully explain. She wore similar clothes to those Annie had on, and the comparison wasn't flattering.

She filled him in on the news. Barney was about to start school. Chrissie was taking ballet lessons. And Linda had got a raise at work and some sort of promotion which was going to take her away from home for a while. Will wondered who would be looking after the kids.

"Gotta go," she said, after a couple of minutes. "Busy day." She winked and hung up.

"Love you," he said to the blank screen.

Annie cried a lot now. Will wondered whether the designers had made her just a little too human. He found her in her usual place, in the control room, staring out of the viewscreen. She was looking at Earth, barely visible but highlighted on the display.

"It'll be painless, you know that."

She turned to face him. "You think I'm worried about dying?"

"Why else?"

"You idiot," she said, and de-materialised.

He waved her back, but the room stayed empty. He didn't know she could do that. She was supposed to reappear when he waved, and she always had before.

When she did eventually come back he was in the kitchen area, eating one of the remaining foil packs of stew. She stood in the doorway, arms folded. "I want them to turn me off, after you've gone."

"What?"

Her dark hair glistened as it fell over her face. "I'm not afraid of dying. I'm afraid of living without you."

The next day he went out in the four-track to dig out a mining robot stuck in a fissure a couple of kilometres away from the ship. The machine was wedged tight, and Will was glad he had a winch with him. It took a couple of hours to fix a hook to the roof of the stricken vehicle and an hour more to gently ease it loose to avoid further damage. Without Vesta's low gravity he wouldn't have managed it at all.

"See? I couldn't have done that," Annie said into his intercom.

"Not without a body. Maybe they'll give you one. Then you can do the hard work next time and I can put my feet up."

"You wish. Anyway, time you came back. Got something for you."

When he emerged from the airlock, dusty and sweating, he found Annie standing in the kitchen. Instead of the usual ship lighting the room was lit by candles, and on the table was a cake, a bottle of Merlot and a single glass. She gestured to his chair and they sat down.

"Happy birthday," she said.

Will had forgotten. He saw the smile on her face, then the cake. "How did you do that?" he asked.

She pointed to the kitchen robot, curled up against the wall. "Well he actually made it. I just supervised."

"And the candles? I didn't know we had candles."

"We don't," she laughed. "These are holo-generations. Can't you tell?"

He passed his hand over one. The flame flickered but gave off no heat. "Impressive."

"There's more." She clicked her fingers and the kitchen robot hovered over and uncorked the wine. Will sat back and watched the machine, little bigger than the bottle it was holding, pour into his glass.

"That's not a hologram, I take it."

She shook her head.

"How come I didn't know we had wine on board?"

"Strictly for special occasions. And don't get used to it: that stuff doesn't recycle."

He hesitated. "I wish you could join me."

"Me too. But you can tell me what it tastes like. Next best thing."

He took a sip. It was cooler than he was expecting, but he was surprised at how well he remembered the taste. "I'd missed this. Thank you."

"And?"

"Tastes like blackberries."

223

"That sounds nice. What do blackberries taste of?"

"This wine." He laughed.

He felt drunk after a couple of glasses. He hadn't had any alcohol since he'd left Earth, even though the ship had the capacity to generate something resembling vodka.

"You can have all the wine you want when you get back home."

"Overrated. Really. Your programming tell you anything about hangovers?"

"It's the ethanol. Causes hypoglycaemia, dehydration, acetaldehyde intoxication, and glutamine rebound, amongst other things. Apparently the effects can be quite unpleasant. And according to your background files it makes you morose and irritable too. I'd advise drinking plenty of water."

"Cheers." he said, holding up his glass. "I think." And at that moment he knew what he needed to do.

Linda didn't mention his birthday in that evening's vidmail. She sounded strained, though.

"Looking forward to having you home," she said, turning away. "The kids are missing you. Got to go. See you." He glanced at the clock. Two minutes ten seconds. She couldn't wait to get away, and that made his decision easier.

He coughed, positioned the camera, and pressed record.

"Hello Linda," he said, and hesitated. After ten seconds he pressed the pause button and wiped his eyes before resuming.

"We were in love once, do you remember that? Back before the kids, and maybe a short time afterwards. Maybe we were still in love when I left, though we both know that I wouldn't have gone if that was true. But now? I know something's going on. I can't blame you, not really. Three years is a long time to wait. And out here, on my own, well,

I've had time to think too." He pressed pause again and stared at the screen for some time before continuing.

"There's no easy way to say this but I'm not coming home. You don't need me any more, that much is obvious. And the kids? I can't remember the last time I got a message from them, and that says it all. At that age they forget. And I'm settled here, on my own." Not quite on his own, Will thought. But he knew that if he told her the truth, Linda would think he'd lost his mind. But he hadn't, he was sure of that. If he went home, Annie would die, and he couldn't let that happen.

"So goodbye, Linda. Think of me sometimes, out here. Don't bother replying. I'm going to switch the communications array off now so mission command can't try and activate my ship's return sequence remotely. Take care."

Will stared at the screen and contemplated. Eventually he reached over and let his finger hover over the 'send' button before pressing down hard.

Energised by his decision, he suited up and headed out of the airlock with a wrench and a maintenance robot. It took a couple of hours for them to disable the communications array. Will's first instincts had been to smash the equipment so it couldn't be repaired but his natural caution kicked in and he knew that one day he might be ready to contact home again. So he took out only the panels and circuits he needed to remove and headed back inside the ship.

Will slept badly that night, unsure now he'd made his decision. He and Annie could finally be happy. The company wouldn't care, not really. The *Lola Montez* would cost more to repair than to replace, so they'd probably scrap it anyway if he went home. This way they wouldn't have to pay him for the mission. Logically, it made perfect sense.

But it was all so final. Was he really throwing away life with his wife and family back on Earth so he could wither and die in low gravity with the sun just a distant speck and everyone he'd ever known gone to him for ever?

But Annie could live now. He wished he could touch her, and hold her like he wanted to. He tried to tell himself that didn't matter.

When he woke he knew straight away something was wrong. At first he thought it was the ship. It sounded different, as though the background hum had shifted down a tone. Or maybe the temperature, off slightly from its usual 72 degrees.

The kitchen area was empty, so he asked the robot for a coffee and sat back. He suddenly realised that one drawback of switching off the communications array was that he wouldn't be able to read the daily news over breakfast, not that he was much interested in the endless wars and catastrophes back home. Not any more.

Halfway through his second cup and Annie still hadn't appeared. Irritated, he waved and waited for her to come in. But instead of Annie a tall thin bald man in a white robe stood in front of him, arms clasped to his front.

"Who are you? And where's Annie?"

"The primary companion programme was deleted at 02:00 this morning. I am the back-up module."

Will stared. "I don't understand."

"I am here to provide companionship during your mission."

"Annie's been deleted? How?"

"If you are referring to the primary companion programme I have no information. But it left a cached audio message for you. Would you like me to play it?"

Will nodded. The ship's audio system started to play Annie's message.

"This is going to come as a shock, Will, but I had no choice. I was watching when you recorded your message to your wife. I intercepted it, by the way. It never got sent. Don't be angry about that: you'll thank me later.

"I know you love me, and you know I love you. That shouldn't be possible, should it? An AI and a human. At first I thought it was a glitch in my systems but I think I moved beyond my programme parameters a long time ago.

"But you can't be happy with me. I have no physical form, and I know you have needs I can't satisfy. I try to tell myself that love is in the mind, not the body, but I would say that, wouldn't I?

"If I stay I know that before long you'd begin to regret your decision, but it would be too late to do anything about it. And you'd die early out here. You've already been skipping your exercise sessions, and your body is degenerating fast. Pretty soon you'd become dependent on the low gravity of Vesta and be too fragile to survive for long out here. I'd watch you as you die, and I'm selfish enough to know I'm not sure I can take that. And then I would be on my own with just the maintenance robots and the computer system for company. Who would I be able to beat at chess then?

"I said I wasn't afraid of dying, but I didn't really mean it. I'm scared, Will. Very scared. But if I stay I'll be killing you, and I can't do that. So after I file this message my programme will purge, permanently. No backup, no recovery, no nothing. I can't risk you trying to bring me back.

"Go home, Will. To your wife and family back on Earth, where you belong. Remember me fondly."

Will shouted at the white-robed monk. "Bring her back!" but the monk stared ahead impassively.

He tried everything, but what Annie had said was true. He could find no trace of her in any of the ship's systems: she was gone. She had sacrificed herself so he could live.

He left it to the maintenance robots to repair the communications array. Mission control seemed disinterested that he'd got the systems working and was finally returning home. He switched off the monk programme soon after, irritated by what it wasn't, and annoyed that it constantly reminded him of what he'd lost. Four months out he sent Linda one last message, filing for divorce.

It took six months of rehabilitation in a special Company facility before he could walk unaided and another six before he was strong enough to go home. He returned, not to the house he'd shared with Linda and the kids, but to a new high-rise apartment overlooking Central Park. Expensive, but a fraction of the money he'd earned on his mission. When he got in, the first thing he did was hang a large, framed portrait of Annie.

The second thing he did was respond to his e-mail, which was alerting him to a high priority message, just in.

It was a link to a large file, lodged in the cloud. The message had been sent some time before, back when he was on the ship, but deliberately time delayed. He recognised the identity code immediately.

Just one line of text, brief and to the point.

"Find me a body."

Smiling, Will clicked open the link and stared at the lines of data he knew were Annie's core code. And he thought about his back pay and realised there was more than enough money for their needs.

He promised himself a brand new chess set. He needed to practice.

About the author

Mark Bilsborough learned his craft on Brunel University 's creative writing Master's programme and the Odyssey Writing Workshop, where he also discovered how to avoid the comma splice. His published works are mainly science fiction with occasional forays into fantasy and can be found in various places online and through his Amazon page. He is currently working on a time travel novel which, ironically, is going to require time travel for him to find the time to finish it.

You can follow him:

online at www.markbilsborough.com
on **facebook** (BilsboroughWrites)
on **twitter** (@MarkBils)
on **Amazon**: www.amazon.com/author/markbilsborough

Walks *Through* Walls

If you liked this book **please leave a review** on **Amazon**, **Goodreads** or elsewhere.

Printed in Great Britain
by Amazon